The Tartan MP3 Player

Book One

Highland Secrets Trilogy

THE TARTAN MP3 PLAYER

HIGHLAND SECRETS

book one

by

C.A. SZAREK

Paper Dragon Publishing

The Tartan MP3 Player
C.A. Szarek

Highland Secrets Book One

Paper Dragon Publishing
North Richland Hills, TX

eBook ISBN: 978-1-941151-04-4
Print book ISBN: 978-1-941151-05-1

Published in the United States of America

First eBook Edition: March, 2014
First Print Edition: April, 2014

Second eBook Edition: July, 2022
Second Print Edition: August, 2022

Third eBook Edition: August, 2023
Third Print Edition: August, 2023

Other Books by C.A. Szarek

<u>Highland Secrets Trilogy & Companions</u>—Historical Fantasy Romance

The Princess and The Laird (Highland Secrets Prequel)

The Tartan MP3 Player (Book One)

The Fae Ring (Book Two)

The Parchment Scroll (Book Three)

Highland Valentine (A Highland Secrets HEA Story)

Highlander's Portrait (A Highland Secrets Story)

<u>Highland Treasures</u>—Historical Fantasy Romance

Highland Oath (Book One)

Highland Essence (Book Two)

Highland Skies (Book Three)

<u>The King's Riders</u>—Fantasy Romance

Sword's Call (Book One)—*Also in Audio*

Love's Call (Book Two)—*Also in Audio*

Rogue's Call (Book Three)—*Also in Audio*

Fate's Call (A Novella from the World of the King's Riders)—*Also in Audio*

<u>Crossing Forces</u>—Romantic Suspense
Collision Force (Book One)—*Also in Audio*
Cole in Her Stocking (A Crossing Forces Christmas)—*FREE read!*
Chance Collision (Book Two)—*Also in Audio*
Calculated Collision (Book Three)—*Also in Audio*
Collision Control (Book Four)—*Also in Audio*
Weekend Collision (A Crossing Forces HEA Story)—*FREE read!*
Superior Collision (Book Five)—*Also in Audio*
Incendiary Collision (Book Six)—*Coming Soon!*

<u>The Giovanni</u>
King of Hearts (Book One)—*Also in Audio*
Queen of Diamonds (Book Two)—*Coming Soon!*

Dedication

chapter one

She was dreaming. *Again.*

Rock music blared from the earbuds in her ears, and Claire ran harder. Somehow the treadmill had more resistance than usual. Felt funny under her feet, too.

Bare feet?

No running shoes?

When she looked down, she jolted. Shock washed over her. Brought her to a screeching halt from her dead run.

She wasn't on a treadmill. Not to mention, she was —

Naked?

Claire didn't have on a stitch of clothing.

"What the hell?"

She wiggled her toes and damp, gritty sand and tiny pebbles squished between them.

"Where the *hell* am I?" Yanking the buds from her ears, she let the wires drape over her shoulders and searched her memory.

Nada.

Panic rose from her gut, and she started to shake all over. Claire sucked in a breath and watched her bare breasts rise and fall.

Frigid sea mist kissed her skin and she shivered.

A beach? Seriously?

What an odd dream.

If she wasn't naked and freezing, it might be pleasant to run on the beach…wherever the heck she was.

She approached the water, but the moment the frigid liquid touched her toes, she jumped back. The scent of salt in the sea spray shook her again.

The ocean?

The sea?

Which one?

She'd never been to the ocean before, so it was a tossup.

Claire's gaze shot skyward when two gulls called to each other. They flew overhead, crossed paths, and then one dove for the water.

Weird, everything's so vivid.

No one was in sight, and neither was any sort of boat or shelter.

Further from the water, the terrain became riddled with cliffs.

She couldn't see over the closest ridge, which sat about six or seven feet high.

A screaming heavy metal song blared from her headphones, clashing with the peaceful morning around her.

At least it *seemed* to be morning.

Clouds littered the sky, covering the sun, but it

wasn't dark out. Her gut said morning, even if she couldn't tell what time it was.

"Okay, Claire. It's cold. Wake up." She backed a few more steps from the water's edge, shaking out her long hair. Her hair tie was gone too.

Claire winced. When her fingertips passed over a tangle, and she had to work it free. Her scalp throbbed.

"Pain. Also feels real."

She jumped up and down in place, trying to warm her chilled body. Her hair skimmed her shoulders and tickled her back, raising gooseflesh from biceps to wrist.

Nothing.

Only the loamy beach. Not the blue walls of her bedroom or the high white ceilings of her little house.

"C'mon, Claire. Wake. Up. Now." She pinched her own forearm. "Damn, ow." Claire rubbed the pulsing spot and looked around. "What the—"

"Who goes there?" A deep, accented voice made her jump.

Her MP3 player crashed to the sand, the wires from her headphones ripping over her shoulders as they flew away from her body, but she didn't go after the devices.

Claire's heart kicked into overdrive, and she shot her arm across her naked breasts. Plastered her palm over her bare sex.

"Okay, don't like this dream anymore." Her voice jumped up an octave.

Why can't I wake up?

Maybe a touch of fright would make her wake the hell up.

"Ummm…hello?" Claire ventured, even though her pulse pounded in her temples. She didn't see the voice's owner, but she was stuck now.

Not like I can run and hide.

She wasn't fond of a stranger seeing her nude, even if gym time had given her a rockin' body.

Claire smirked. Her sister would've declared her egotistical right then and there.

Three figures came into view, standing atop a grassy overhang and staring down at her. Two men and a boy.

"Lass?" one asked.

Lass?

Okay, no more Scottish Highlander romance novels before bed for you, Claire McGowan. At least she'd placed the accent.

All three were dressed in period clothing. Like — seventeen hundreds or something. The tallest one had a tartan plaid on.

The man who'd spoken was older, wearing a thick gray beard he was currently scratching, as if he was trying to figure her out.

Well, duh. Naked girl on the beach at the ass crack of dawn should do it every time.

The boy looked about ten. He scrambled down the incline, stopping about three feet from her and staring.

Wide blue eyes. Dark, messy hair that needed a good cut.

Claire backed up, squeezing her eyes shut. "Seriously, wake up." Although, she *should* pat herself on the back for the vivid imagination—if she didn't have to cover her tender parts—she would've *so* been on that.

This place looked and *felt* real.

"Are ye Fae?" The kid's brogue was thick, but his voice was high, making him sound younger than she'd guessed.

"Wh-what?" Claire asked, taking another step back.

"Angus, hush," the last man admonished. His voice was familiar; he'd been the one who'd called out first. He jumped down to the beach with little effort.

Claire almost forgot to cover herself as she gazed *up* at him.

Had to be about six-five or six-six.

Definitely had a foot on her, for sure.

Blue eyes, like the kid. Long dark hair—nearly black—flowing in the wind. He was the one wearing a kilt, and had the same tartan pattern strewn across his body, shoulder to waist and held down with a belt, a puffy-sleeved ivory shirt beneath it, but it was open at the neck. Dark chest hair peeked out and her stomach fluttered.

Good job, Claire. At least you dreamt up someone yummy.

The model on the cover of the book she'd been reading before bed had *nothing* on this guy.

"Lass? Are ye well?" His voice was concerned, as was his expression. He spoke gently.

"M-m-m-me?"

Way to go on the stutter, Clair-bear.

Her sister's nickname for her popped into her head with ease. It should've grounded her, but she still didn't wake up.

"She speaks funny, Uncle!"

How can he tell?

She'd said two words, literally.

"Where am I?" Claire whispered. The sinking feeling in the pit of her stomach made her shift on her feet.

"Isle of Skye." The boy jumped up and down. "We were s'ppose ta go fishing. But I found ye, instead."

"Hush, Angus MacLeod," the man said, but there was amusement in his tone. However, he didn't take his eyes off Claire.

A tremor slid down her spine when his gaze traveled her frame.

Still. Naked.

She wanted to sink into the sand, her earlier confidence about her body gone. Claire shivered; her teeth chattered.

"Jesu, lass. Yer freezin'." The huge man unbelted the plaid from his waist and whipped the shirt off his torso. Now he stood before her bare-chested. His accent was as thick as the boy's, but she could make his words out better.

Sexy as hell.

"Yeah, kinda naked over here." A nervous titter fell from her lips and made her wince.

"Is she Fae, Uncle?" Angus asked.

"Ye've been spendin' too much time wit' my father." The man laughed, but it had a nervous edge. He called to the older man on the ridge. "Da, stop cloudin' the lad's head with faery tales."

The older guy on the hill chuckled. "Och, then dinnae leave the lad wit' me when ye go off."

"Like I have a choice."

Claire's focus scattered when he threw his shirt over her shoulders. She struggled into the huge garment, and warmth enveloped her, as well as his clean masculine scent.

Sandalwood and fresh peat. Earthy, yet delicious.

Like he'd stepped out of her damn book.

All she could see in front of her was a wide expanse of bare, well-defined chest. His arms and pecs were *huge*.

She stopped counting abs when she got to four on each side. There was a dark strip of hair dividing his eight-pack and disappearing into that kilt.

Claire had to swallow hard.

Gorgeous didn't even cover it. She forbade herself from wondering what he had *under* the tartan.

"There, lass. Are ye hale?" He rubbed her arms up

and down on the outside of the fabric.

She clutched the huge shirt closer at the neck, since it was big and immediately wanted to go off-shoulder. She fought a shiver that had nothing to do with the chill of the beach.

Their eyes locked, and one corner of his mouth shot up.

"I'm good. Thanks." She forced words out. Claire's mouth went dry. Her tongue was thick, stuck to her palate.

He paused, as if he was trying to make sense of her words. Then he nodded. "Duncan MacLeod." He inclined his head and smiled.

"Like the TV show from the nineties?" she blurted. *Way to be original in dreamland.*

On the other hand, she'd loved that show.

"What, lass?" He cocked his head to one side, studying her like the kid standing beside him still was.

"Nothing." Claire shook her head.

"She *is* Fae, Uncle."

Duncan MacLeod sighed and crossed his arms over his massive — still naked — chest. "Angus, another word an' I'm goin' ta make ye join yer grandfa."

The boy jumped up and down. "But Uncle, look a' her. Fair hair, like my—"

The man clamped a hand over the kid's mouth. He grabbed him up against his broad torso, his little feet dangling above the ground. "Enough, lad."

With a dramatic sigh, Angus deflated and nodded.

Duncan MacLeod set him to his feet.

The kid stared up at him, visibly disappointed, his little shoulders caved in.

"Up the hill, wit' yer grandfa."

He didn't speak, as he obeyed. He dashed to the overhang and scrambled up like a gold medal rock climber. "Sorry, Uncle," he muttered when he was about halfway.

"I'm sorry, lass. He's…"

"Fine." Claire had to smile. The kid was cute. "A normal little boy."

When Duncan MacLeod grinned, her heart stuttered. "Da, take Angus back ta Dunvegan. Tell Janey ta have a warm bath ready, an' somethin' fer the lass ta wear. A meal, too. We'll join ye shortly."

"What? No…" Claire shook her head.

"Nay, lass. Ye'll do as I say." He glanced up to the ridge.

She snapped her mouth shut.

His tone brooked no argument.

Hey, is this my dream, or what?

This didn't feel like a dream anymore. Not that it ever really had.

Duncan's father nodded, resting a hand on the kid's shoulders. "See ye, then." The old man waved.

Claire shifted on her feet under the weight of Duncan's gaze, when the others had left them.

"Now, lass. Ye an' I shall speak. Who are ye, an' where did ye come from?"

chapter two

"This is a dream. This *has* to be a dream, right?"

Duncan MacLeod's sapphire eyes searched her face, and he settled his large hands on her upper arms. "A dream?"

Through the linen material of his shirt, the heat of his grip sank into her body. Claire's limbs tingled.

"The lad was right, ye do speak…oddly," he muttered, but he was talking more to himself than her.

She cleared her throat as panic started to rise from her belly. "This isn't a dream. Oh my God. I'm in Scotland. My trip…" Her legs wobbled; her vision wavered.

"Aye, Scotland. On my lands—Clan MacLeod. On tha Isle of Skye, in tha Hebrides."

Shit. I'm gonna pass out.

"Lass?" Duncan's voice held concern, but his eyes, then his handsome face blurred.

She couldn't focus. Black crept up and Claire's muscles let go.

"Lass?"

Warmth enveloped her and she sucked in a breath. She was up against something—someone—solid. She sucked in air and moaned. Her temples throbbed.

Am I finally awake?

"Lass?"

Claire refused to open her eyes. The sound of rushing waters made her whimper.

The beach.

The man.

Duncan MacLeod.

"You keep calling me that."

"Ye have yet ta tell me what yer called, s'all." When the laugh rumbled against her body, as well as greeted her ears, her eyes flew open.

Claire was in his arms. Against his massive chest. Her belly warmed. Desire made her throb between her legs.

Desire?

You don't even know this guy.

Yeah, but he's holding me entirely off the ground. Strong arms. Muscles galore. Plus, he's hot as hell.

Talking to herself?

Answering herself?

Maybe Claire was in a coma.

In a mental institution.

She was going crazy.

"Are ye well? Ye...seem ta have the vapors."

The vapors?

What the hell?

"I'm good. I'm okay. You can let go of me." She met his blue eyes, read doubt there. "Promise. I'm good."

"From where do ye hale, lass? What're ye called?" Duncan put her to her feet, but didn't take his large hands off her.

Claire didn't pull away, either. She met his gaze and cleared her throat. "Texas. Claire. Claire McGowan."

"Texas?" Duncan struggled with the word. "Where's that?"

"Umm…you know, the US…United States of America?"

"America? The new world," Duncan breathed.

A chill shot down her spine and she stared at his chest, his kilt, then the beach around them. She clutched Duncan's shirt closer around her neck. "The new world?" she whispered.

"Em, aye. The English. They've colonies. I've heard a' such a place. Never been. Nary a desire ta go away from my homeland." He said the word *English*, as if it was an insult.

Jesus, this isn't a dream.

Claire's head spun, and her heart kicked up a notch. "Oh. My. God."

"Claire?"

Her name on Duncan's lips made her eyes shoot to his again. She couldn't even take a second to enjoy his sexy brogue. Tremors racked her frame. She broke their physical contact.

She started to pace, holding his shirt tight to her

body. She shook her head. "This isn't possible."

"What, lass?" His expression was as confused as she felt.

"No. Way. Just—no fricking way."

"Lass. Claire. Look a' me." Duncan grabbed her, but he didn't hurt her.

Claire obeyed, as if compelled, and swallowed. Hard. His handsome face was open, waiting for whatever she had to say.

Hot or not, she wished for the dream she thought she'd been having when she'd come to, running on the beach.

Then she could simply have her way with him and wake up in her own bed afterwards. Yes, a wet dream would be preferable to the math that was adding up in her head.

"Duncan." His name fell from her lips and her stomach twisted, as her mind fought for understanding.

Nothing made sense.

"Claire." Duncan's voice was calm. Waiting. "Tell me."

"I think I traveled back in time."

Duncan searched a pair of leaf-green eyes as the lass quaked in his grip. He saw no deceit.

There was only one way she could've done what

she'd said.

The Faery Stones.

The very magic he'd been searching for—for the last six months.

His heart thumped.

Was this lass a clue to finding Alex?

"Claire." Her name rolled off his tongue with ease. She was beautiful.

His laddie had thought she was Fae, and she could pass for it. Flaxen locks, long and wavy, fair flawless complexion and green, *green* eyes. However, Duncan's instinct said she wasn't.

When her eyes came back to his, his pulse thundered in his ears. He wanted to make her feel better. Hold her close like he had when she'd fainted. Cup her face and dip his mouth down to taste her.

He jolted. Duncan had no business wanting to kiss her.

Where was that coming from?

Of course, he'd always appreciated a bonnie lass, but desiring to taste one he'd just met was a bit much, even for him. Besides, it hadn't been so long since he'd had a woman. Perhaps he needed to visit the widow.

She'd been his only lover in recent years, as she was barren. There were several whores aboard the ship, but he'd never paid them attention. Duncan wouldn't risk having any bastards.

He wasn't going anywhere—including back to sea, until he figured out the beauty before him.

Claire looked lost, and his gut tightened.

He squeezed her slender shoulders. "How did ye come ta the beach?"

"I don't know. I...came to, and I was running."

"Ye came to?" Duncan listened carefully. Her words weren't so different from his, but her accent was foreign. Like no other he'd ever heard.

"I...thought I was dreaming. But...all the sand...beach...even seagulls. Then I realized I was naked."

God's Blood, she was, and gloriously so. Every inch of the woman's body was beautiful.

Duncan's cock twitched, and he threatened to lop it off.

Now wasn't the time.

Seeing Claire wearing his oversized leine was appealing on a level it shouldn't be. He wanted to take it off her...warm her another way.

"What's the last thing ye remember?"

She tilted her head, then panic shot across her pretty visage. "Oh. My. God. I can't remember *anything* else." Her eyes widened. "Why aren't you freaked out about all this?"

"Freaked out?"

Claire stomped her small foot in the sand. "I just told you I came through time, and you don't even look rattled. I'm from the *future*."

Duncan nodded. "I believe ye, lass."

Shock rolled over her expression, and she shook

her head. "How? Why? *I* don't believe me."

He laughed and was almost overwhelmed with the urge to kiss her again when her pink tongue darted out to moisten her plump bottom lip. He swallowed a groan.

Not now.

Not e'er.

"Tell me the last thing ye remember."

"I…" Claire shook her head and trembled under his hands.

"C'mere. Lass. Claire." Duncan couldn't watch her struggle. He drew her into his arms.

She nestled into his chest without hesitation. "Why can't this just be a dream?" Her words were muffled, but he couldn't focus on that.

The lass didn't come up to his shoulders. This slight, slender woman fit up against him as if she belonged.

Her soft to his hard, touching him in all the right places.

It was Duncan's turn to shiver, but he fought it. He wanted to kiss the top of her fair head but didn't. He held her, rubbing her back atop the fabric of his leine, wishing it was her bare skin he touched.

When Claire squared her shoulders against him, Duncan released her.

The lass was ready to talk.

"I'm okay."

Good, she's strong.

"I was reading a book. In bed, in a cottage I guess can't be too far away." Claire looked away, and her cheeks reddened, but then she met his gaze.

"Ye read?"

"Of course, I can read." Annoyance flashed through her green eyes, and Duncan bit back a smile.

She was strong and stubborn; suddenly even more appealing.

"Most women dinnae read, unless they're noble. Are ye noble, Claire? Ye said MacGowan? I'm unfamiliar with your clan."

"It's M-c, not M-a-c. I'm American. And I don't have a clan. My time…is different than yours." She darted about five feet away and bent to the sand to retrieve something. "Damn," Claire muttered.

"Somethin' wrong?" Duncan joined her and stared at the item in her hands.

"My MP3 player. It's either broken or the battery's dead." She wiped off the small rectangular thing.

"Yer what?"

"It's…never mind." Claire shook her head.

He made a grab for it, and she let him take it. He turned the thing over and over in his hands. It was hard. Made of no material he was familiar with.

It had a little silver cross on the front, with arrows etched in all four directions. Above the cross-like thing was a black box that felt different under his thumb than the rest of the thing.

The face and back were covered in blue, red and

green plaid, but it wasn't cloth; it was painted on the surface of the item.

"Clan MacGowan plaid? I dinnae recognize it."

"Uh, no. No clan, like I said. It's just a skin. I…like plaid."

"Skin?"

Claire made a face and grabbed the thing from his grip. "Never mind. It's not like I can charge it here."

"Nay, howe'er, 'tis proof a yer words bein' true."

Their gazes collided.

"Yer in my time, lass." Duncan's heart gave a funny thud when her green eyes misted over.

"That's what I was afraid of."

chapter three

"Okay, so the bath isn't so bad." She sighed and reclined into the back of the giant wooden tub, glancing around the room. There was a piece of cloth, or linen, like a sheet, as wet as she, since it lined the tub. Probably to keep from getting splinters in one's ass.

Handy.

She glanced around the place—Duncan's room.

Claire shivered, and it had nothing to do with the hot water caressing her body. She rested her arms on the top of the tub, at the edges, tilting her head back and closing her eyes against the scenery of intricately carved, dark wood, oversized furniture.

Turned out Duncan was the laird—the head of the clan. Claire knew what the title meant. She'd been obsessed with anything Scottish Highlander for years.

Too bad her romance novel fetish wasn't doing anything to help her very odd—*unbelievable*—situation.

She just kept picturing Duncan naked in the huge bed she was pretending not to notice.

He wasn't married, so his sister kept the castle in order.

Janey—Janet MacLeod—was tall, buxom, and

gorgeous. Dark hair and blue eyes—basically the female version of Duncan.

"I've got ye a skirt an' a leine ta wear. Hope they fit. I'm a bit taller than ye. Here's a chemise, too." Duncan's sister smiled and held up a sleeveless garment that'd probably go to Claire's ankles. It looked soft, ivory linen, like a nightgown.

The other woman rested a navy skirt and white shirt-looking thing, on a nearby chair. The material of the skirt was thick—probably wool. It'd be heavy.

Janet's words were a little clearer somehow, but she still had a thick Scottish Highland brogue.

"A what?"

"Ye mean the leine? A tunic, I suppose. Ye know that term?" The pretty woman's smile was kind, but she didn't seem the least bit phased that Claire was so *foreign*.

Had Duncan told her about the time travel?

"Yes. Thank you." Claire returned the smile and shifted in the tub.

Janet might be female, but Claire wasn't any fonder of showing her nudity to Duncan's sister than she had been to him. At least she was efficient about it. Her eyes never landed anywhere other than on Claire's face.

"Call me when yer ready ta dress, an' I'll help ye lace the bodice." Janet patted a navy-blue corset and Claire groaned.

She'd worn one for a Renaissance faire once, and it

did nothing but leave her with sore boobs. However, with no bra, she didn't have much of a choice. "Thank you."

Duncan's sister nodded and bustled about the room for a moment. "Need anythin' else lass? I'll have the kitchen fix ye somethin' to eat?"

"I'm good, but thank you, once again." Nerves fluttered in Claire's stomach. "I feel like all I'm doing is thanking you, but I mean it."

"'Tis nothin'." Janet flashed a wide smile that made her look so much like her older brother Claire's heart sped up.

A knock sounded on the door, but Duncan didn't pause before entering the room.

"Get out, Duncan MacLeod!" Janet rushed forward. "The lady is nay clothed."

"I need ta speak wit' Claire."

"'Tis nothin' that dinnae need wait!" His sister blocked the view with her body, but Duncan pushed passed her.

"It's okay," Claire said, but Janet didn't stop yelling.

She smirked. The *conversation* was reminiscent of Claire's own big sister, Jules, nagging her about something or another.

Duncan ignored Janet, coming closer to the tub.

Heat crept up Claire's neck and settled into her cheeks. She sank down into the water, but it was cloudy from Janet's soap anyway. Adequately hid her private parts.

Not that he hadn't already seen them down on the beach.

Duncan's sister fussed for a moment, then threw her hands up. "I'll take my leave an' get the lass some bread and cheese, but *ye* leave this room, Duncan MacLeod. Dinnae be proper."

Taking the only other empty seat in the large room, he ignored Janet, and she slipped away, shutting the door with a soft *thud*.

"Umm…"

"Dinnae mind me, lass. Get warm. When ye need ta dress, I'll turn away from ye."

Claire nodded and swallowed again—for what felt like the hundredth time that day. His blue stare scorched, warmed her skin, as if he'd touched her.

She wanted him to touch her.

Knock it off.

"What's so urgent?" Claire made herself force words out.

His expression was grave, and Duncan nodded. "Aye. Nay further delay."

"What is it?"

"I need yer help, lass."

"My help?" The lass's fair brows were drawn tight, and Duncan shifted in his seat.

How on earth could he explain everything so she'd believe him?

Claire coming from another time might make it even more difficult.

Will she understand?

He needed to find the Faery Stones so he could get Alex back from the Fae Realm, and the clutches of the Scottish Fae King Fillan. Six long months, and he'd gone to all the isles of the Hebrides. Scouring all the places the pirate's seer recommended.

The blasted woman had been wrong so far.

Did Claire's arrival mean something?

Could this lass from another time help him find and free his brother—and his Fae princess wife?

Alex was the true Laird of the MacLeods.

Duncan cleared his throat. "What do ye ken of the Faery Stones?"

"Faery? Like what Angus said? Something about Fae?" Claire's fair brows were drawn tight, and he could almost feel her confusion.

He wanted to smooth her frown, cup her cheeks, and kiss her lips. Taste her—

Not now, Duncan Roderick Iain MacLeod.

"Aye. As the lad said."

Claire straightened in the bathing tub. The tops of her breasts peeked out of the water, and Duncan made himself look away. Tried to ignore the memory of her bared before him on the beach.

"I've heard the term 'Fae' in books I've read.

But…none of it's real. It's all fairy tales. Stuff to scare kids. Like the Boogey Man."

Duncan arched an eyebrow. "Boogey Man?"

"Uhh…a guy who hides in the closet or under the bed and gets you in the dark."

He chuckled. "Ne'er heard such a thing. But we've the tale of the banshee. Her cry bursts yer ears." Especially when a man mistreated a woman, at least, according to his mother. Duncan smirked at the memory. He missed his mother, who'd passed some ten years before.

"Yeah, Phoebe turned into one on the original *Charmed* once."

He stared, as he processed the unfamiliar words.

Claire's pretty face went pink, and she shook her head. "Never mind."

Duncan couldn't look away from her appealing blush. The lass was tempting. She was naked in his room. He shifted on the chair and ignored his twitching cock. "Dinnae fash, lass."

"Claire."

"What?"

"You can call me Claire. May I call you Duncan, or do you prefer 'my laird?'"

Duncan shook his head. "Duncan. I'm no' tha laird."

"What? But Janet said—"

"Aye. 'Tis temporary. Our older brother, Alex, is Laird of Clan MacLeod."

Claire stared and Duncan chided himself to gather his words quickly and efficiently.

"Angus' father?"

"Aye." He nodded, his gut tightening just thinking about his situation. Duncan had never desired the responsibility of running his clan. Never envied Alex's position of birth or destiny.

When their mother's health had required a change of the guard, and their father had stepped down to care for his wife, Alex had stepped up, as his birthright had demanded.

Duncan had also ensured he'd be there for his clan and family any way he could, and he had been. He'd just never foreseen his brother marrying a Fae princess in secret and having a child with her.

Angus had shown up in a basket with a note some nine years ago, as a tiny brand-new laddie, but it had all been a ruse. His sister, only a slip of a lass then, had helped the Princess Alana deliver her bairn.

Duncan and his father had been witness to the clandestine wedding of Alex and his princess in the chapel of Dunvegan, so Angus had been born in wedlock, but the rest of Clan MacLeod assumed the lad was a bastard by a whore.

Unfortunately, they treated him as such, except his immediate family, of course. Angus was Alex's heir, and would be laird someday, as was his birthright.

No one knew Alana and Alex were married—or that she visited them as often as she could. The location of the Faery Stones—her method of transport to their world—was secret even from Alex himself.

Alana's father, the Fae King Fillan, had discovered their secret and nabbed Alex. Duncan felt in his gut his brother was still alive, but he wouldn't be for much longer. He'd been a captive for six months.

Angus had Fae magic. His mother had come to him in a dream and told him to alert Duncan. They were both imprisoned.

The king planned to put Alex to death and was holding Alana against her will for betraying him and his plans. The princess had been betrothed to a Fae prince.

The lad had been frantic for both his parents.

Duncan had started the search the following morning—yielding nothing so far, or in the frustrating intervening months.

"The Fae might be in tales, but they're verra real, Claire."

She scoffed, and water shifted with her movements, splashing against the side of the tub.

"Ye've come through time, yet ye doubt?"

Claire paused; her green eyes boring into him. "True. I was still hoping this is all a dream."

Duncan smirked. "Nay, lass."

"So, the Fae—or faeries or whatever—are real?" Her tone was a combination of curiosity and disbelief.

"Aye, an' they hold my brother captive."

chapter four

►► "Why? What happened?"

"Angus *happened.*" Duncan scratched his head.

Claire stared.

His cheeks were flushed, and he shifted his large form on the chair. He was visibly uncomfortable. It didn't give his incredible words any credence.

"What?"

"My brother found himself in love wit' a Fae princess an' married her in secret. My da an' I were witness. Angus was born shortly thereafter. Alana left the lad here tha day a' his birth, as it's obvious ta the Fae he's half human, an' they wish ta harm him. She dinnae be able ta keep him safe and ken we would. Her father discovered them an' took Alex."

"Your nephew's a fairy?" Claire blinked.

"Weel, a halfling. The Fae dinnae be fond of such creatures. His mother's people wish him dead. So, Alex, an' my sister, our da, an' I, are raisin' him. 'Til Alana can come, if tha' day e'er arrives." Duncan drew his hand down his face, as if what he'd said had bothered him for a long time.

What kind of people killed little kids?

How can any of this be true?
Then again, Claire *had* traveled through time.
She shook her head.
Duncan rose from the chair and came to the tub, taking one of her hands in his as she gazed up at him. "'Tis all true, Claire. An' I need yer help."
Heat suffused her cheeks at his closeness — and her nudity. "How...how...can *I* help you? Until today, I didn't believe in any of this stuff."
"Ye came ta my time through the Faery Stones."
"I did? How do you know?"
"There's nay another way, nay other magic. Ye have ta help me find the Stones. I have ta get my brother back. An' Alana. Fer Angus. Fer my clan, my family."
Magic?
Claire sputtered, looking down into the cloudy water before she could meet Duncan's imploring blue eyes. "I need to get out of the tub. Water's cold," she blurted.
His expression shouted that was the last thing he thought she'd say, but the temporary laird nodded and released her hand, taking a step back. "A' course."
Their gazes collided.
They both froze.
"Um, can you turn? So, I can stand?"
Duncan jumped, and Claire's cheeks burned.
"Aye."
She watched his impossibly broad shoulders shift when his back faced her. He'd put on a white tunic, and

it was tucked into the kilt, a wide leather belt around his waist.

His calves were pure muscle and sprinkled with springy black hair, but it wasn't a turn off. Duncan's feet were encased in the deer hide boots she'd read about in many a book. His long dark hair settled down, his back in waves her fingers itched to touch.

Damn, even with his back turned, the man dripped sex.

A tremor shot down her spine as she rose on wobbly legs to exit the tub.

"All is well, Claire?"

The way he said her name made her want to melt.

She cleared her throat and dived for the chemise. "Yes." Claire shoved her arms through the garment and smoothed it over her breasts, down her body. It landed at her ankles, as suspected, and was soft as butter. Detailed with pretty lace at the low neckline. "You can turn around."

Duncan's eyes widened when he looked at her. "Put on the leine, lass."

"Why?"

A smile played at his lips and his Adam's apple bobbed. "Dinnae be complainin' but I can see through yer chemise."

"Oh!" Claire jumped, her cheeks and neck flaming all over again. She grabbed the tunic, plastering it in front of her body.

He chuckled. "Dinnae be fashed, Claire-lass. Yer a

bonnie lass."

Duncan thinks I'm beautiful.

Claire's heart thundered. Her fingers were frozen to the fabric of the leine. It wasn't as soft as the chemise, but it was a light material.

The distraction in her hands wasn't enough to tear her focus from the attraction sizzling between them. It was palpable, like lightening zinging all over her body, warming her limbs, settling in her lower belly.

Duncan's gaze bored into her, and he took a step closer.

She could feel the heat coming off his large form.

When he reached, she moved into his fingertips, instead of away.

He caressed her cheek, but he didn't lean down to kiss her.

Claire tilted her face up, sending a silent invitation, then stilled, chiding herself.

You met him today.

It didn't matter.

She yearned for his mouth on hers.

Duncan grabbed a strand of her hair, dragging his fingers down its length, but he didn't tug. His eyes were heavy-lidded. Although he said nothing, his breathing was rough.

Kiss me.

After a few heartbeats, he stepped back, muttering something under his breath. It wasn't English.

"What?" Claire whispered.

"Nay, Claire-lass." Duncan smiled. "Talking ta myself."

"Gaelic?"

"Aye. Ye speak my tongue?"

Don't say tongue. I want to wrap mine around yours.

Claire cleared her throat. "No, sorry. I speak some Spanish, though."

One dark eyebrow arched. "What need do ye have ta speak wit' a Spaniard?"

She smirked. "Well, where I live, they're not from Spain, and there's much need." Claire wasn't even going to try to explain Mexico and Texas to him.

"Then I'm glad ye have the skill."

She nodded, forcing her arms into the puffy long sleeves of the leine. She pulled it over her head and tugged it down. She liked the loose fit, but groaned when she remembered the constricting bodice. "Can you call Janet?" Claire asked. "She said she would help me lace the corset."

"I can help ye." The wicked grin on Duncan's face told her how many times he'd helped a woman *unlace* one.

She frowned. "Um, that's okay. It's…"

"Lass, I want ta help."

Before Claire could comment, Duncan had her arms in the proper place, and wrapped the stiff bodice around her.

He began to lace up the back without a word, working deftly and gently, considering she was being trussed up.

"Thanks."

"'Tis nay a bother, Claire. Yer in my time, my castle. I'm responsible fer ye now."

She glanced over her shoulder. "No, you're not."

"Aye. I am." Duncan's tone brooked no argument, like when they'd been down on the beach, so she dropped the subject and focused on the feel of his hands working where she couldn't see.

Heat.

She was surrounded in warmth, even though he wasn't touching her bare skin. Claire wanted him to brush her whole—naked—body with his large hands.

She imagined what it would feel like to have his lips on the back of her neck. Duncan nibbling on her ear.

Claire shivered.

"Lass, are ye well? Did I hurt ye?"

Knock it off.

You just *met this guy.*

"I'm fine. Thank you for helping me."

Crap.

She'd already thanked him.

Oversized hands landed on her shoulders and turned her.

Claire raised her eyes and met Duncan's.

He smiled, and her stomach fluttered. "Yer welcome." His sapphire orbs traveled her frame.

She trembled in his grip, but not from fear. How

could she *want* someone she'd met less than three hours before?

The leine fell mid-thigh, so she wasn't physically exposed to him, but he devoured her with one look, and her body responded.

Warmed. Her core throbbed.

"Claire." Her name was a whisper, and her heart stuttered.

Disappointment flooded her when his hands fell away from her shoulders, and he took a step back.

Duncan cleared his throat. "I'll leave ye ta finish dressin'."

"You don't have to go." Claire's words were rushed. "I mean, you can show me to my room, or whatever." Her cheeks burned for the hundredth time since she'd met Duncan MacLeod.

He's gonna think I'm an idiot.

"Ye'll stay with me, a'course."

"Here?" Claire croaked. She gestured to the huge bed.

"Aye."

"But—"

"I'll no' harm ye, lass."

"But..." Claire swallowed a wince as intelligent words refused to exit her mouth.

Duncan smirked.

Oh, God. I'm in so much trouble.

chapter five

Duncan left the lass in his room. 'Twas for the best he walk away. Or he might have helped her *out* of the bodice, he'd just taken the time to thread and tighten.

He wanted the lass—couldn't deny it even to himself.

Hungered to taste her lips, touch her body, lie with her in his own bed. The fact that Claire had tilted her face up in invitation could get him in trouble.

Maybe he should go see the widow.

Nay.

Now that he'd met Claire McGowan, the vision of Meg naked didn't stir him.

Duncan shook his head and growled to himself. He needed to meet with Riley O'Malley in the caves anyway. The slimy Irish pirate was doing him a favor by letting him captain his ship, *the Fancy Seer,* but it wasn't without cost.

Riley—and his ilk—required coin as well as safe passage through MacLeod waters.

If he were a betting man, Duncan would assume Riley O'Malley was planning on entry into the Realm of the Fae to try his hand at gaining Faery riches.

He had no intention of confirming or denying. Duncan needed Alex back. If Riley O'Malley got himself killed by Fae Warriors, it was no matter to him.

The soldier class of the Fae was made up of winged gods, fantastic with any weapon they yielded. Legend said they could sense when a human stepped foot in their realm.

Duncan hadn't dwelt on it too much, though he feared they would be in for a fight when they finally found the Stones. He'd met a Fae Warrior several times; a huge man named Xander, who was protector and kin to his brother's princess. The man hadn't had wings when he'd been present at the wedding, but he'd been told it was due to the lack of magic in what Alana had called the Human Realm.

Had the princess' cousin been captured as well?

The man had seemed to care for Alana and wouldn't appreciate her being locked up.

Duncan *would* get his brother back.

Could the Fae man help his quest?

Too bad there was no way to contact Xander or Alex, for that matter.

They were to sail in mere days. Before they'd left on their first journey some six months before, Riley had gained a new crew so everyone would believe Duncan the captain, and not question their mission.

Riley's seer—and lover—Bridei, was supposedly part Fae, but she was a fraud, as far as Duncan was concerned. He'd had no results from the woman.

Angus would be able to tell if she was actually Fae, but he wouldn't risk the lad by letting the pirates close, especially since he'd barely seen his family or his home since Alex had been gone.

This was Duncan's first time home in a month. The pirate captain had insisted on a break in their grueling pace. His men needed more than the two or three whores on ship.

Riley O'Malley had insisted on a trip home — to the Emerald Isle, as he called Ireland. *The Fancy Seer* had made its way back to Skye only two days before.

"Duncan."

"Nay, Da. I'm late." He tried to push past his father as he made his way across the great hall, but the older man grabbed his arm.

"Lad, listen."

He met blue eyes that matched his own.

Iain MacLeod was no longer the laird — having stepped down when he'd felt that his wife's poor health had demanded it years before, but his father's grip and stare were a command. He'd also changed from the trews, and leine he'd worn on the beach when they'd found Claire. He was dressed in a plaid, like Duncan, and his silvering dark hair was damp. He must've bathed.

Too bad his mother had passed on, before Angus was born.

They all still mourned Lady Caitriona.

He refused to let that happen to his brother, too.

"What?" Duncan tried not to snap. Chided himself to show the respect the man who'd raised him deserved.

"The lass' arrival 'tis a sign, lad."

Duncan shifted in his boots and gave a curt nod. "I'll find Alex."

"I ken it." Iain nodded and released him. "Now go but be quick an' discreet."

"Aye. As always. Where's Angus?"

"Yer sister managed ta sit him down fer a meal."

"Good. Tell her ta keep him busy. I'll dinnae have him following me ta the cliffs." Duncan left his father in the great hall, striding across the bailey and mulling over his words.

Maybe it was as his father believed.

Claire's arrival from another time was a sign.

Did it mean he was close to getting his brother back?

He quickened his step.

Duncan talked himself out of reaching over his shoulder to grip on the hilt of the claymore strapped to his back as soon as his feet hit the wide deck of *the Fancy Seer*. He wasn't in danger, even if his skin crawled when he'd boarded.

She was hidden well inside a huge watery cave. The narrowness of the strait-like area attested to the skill of the pirate Riley O'Malley, and Duncan hated that.

A lesser sailor could've run the vessel aground on

the sharp rocks that surrounded them.

The men that skittered by him, going about their tasks, wouldn't meet his eyes, but that was fine with Duncan, as long as they saw him as captain and gave him the appropriate respect.

"Where's my first mate?" he barked.

"Yer quarters, Captain."

Duncan thanked him but growled under his breath.

Of course, the slimy bastard couldn't maintain the charade with him home on Skye. He'd have to cleanse the place before taking it over again.

Duncan wasn't afraid to get dirty, but lying in Riley's bed made his skin crawl.

The feminine moans greeted his ears even before he pushed his way in what was supposed to be *his* refuge on *The Fancy Seer*.

He opened the door, bracing himself for what he was about to see.

Bridei's back was arched, her dark hair flowing free down her slender back as she rode her man on the bed *Duncan* was supposed to sleep on.

Riley had his head tilted up, long scraggly red hair loose, eyes closed while his woman serviced him.

Duncan cleared his throat, tapping his booted foot to the dirty planked floor.

The pirate captain's head flew up, eyes wide. When he saw Duncan, his shoulders relaxed into the bed. A wide grin spread on his face, and he grabbed one of Bridei's breasts. "Look, love, the laird likes ta watch."

The Irish inflection made Duncan want to frown. He'd never disliked anyone from Ireland before — until he'd met this man and his ilk.

Bridei threw a seductive look over her shoulder that roiled his stomach. "Maybe he'll finally join us." Her voice was deep for a woman's. She licked already kiss-swollen lips.

Duncan ignored the seer's beckoning hand.

"Yer late," Riley drawled. He rested his hands on his woman's rounded hips, stopping her undulating. However, he didn't push her off him, nor did he exit the bed.

Duncan narrowed his eyes, praying for control. He wanted to run the pirate captain through. "I need a few days. Somethin' has come up."

Riley arched an auburn eyebrow. "Oh?"

"'Tis none of yer concern. Stay docked here, an' I'll come ta ye when I'm ready. I assume ye've supplies enough to sail?"

The pirate captain scowled. "Yer wastin' my time."

"I paid fer yer time," Duncan barked.

"It'll cost ye more, for every day we're delayed."

"Fine." He loosed the purse on his belt and tossed it to the slimy bastard. "Get yer arse out of *my* quarters, and by God's Blood, get new linens on the bed."

Bridei looked him up and down, making no move to hide her nudity. She caressed her own breasts, then her stomach. Her hand froze on its journey downward when Duncan threw her a black look.

She wasn't ugly—her breasts were large and high, and her skin had an attractive olive tone. She was slender and rounded where it counted, but she made his skin crawl. Not to mention, he'd always preferred fair hair.

Like Claire.

He made eye contact with Riley and heard the seer mutter, "Yer loss."

"Have yer woman concentrate more on tha likely location of tha Stones, an' less on tha stick between yer legs."

Riley smirked. "Aye, Captain." He must be content with the additional coin in his palm—for now.

Duncan ignored the mocking in his voice. As long as Riley feigned the appropriate respect when they had an audience, he'd accept disrespect in private.

How much longer could he manage dealing with Riley O'Malley and pirate rubbish?

God, let me be close to finding Alex.

chapter six

Claire was asleep by the time Duncan made it back to his quarters. He'd bought himself a few days to figure out what her arrival could mean. He'd have to talk to the steward, Hamish, and account for the coin he'd need from MacLeod coffers for O'Malley, but he'd deal with it when he had to.

Greedy bastard pirate.

The peat in the hearth had burned down, but his rooms held warmth.

Duncan removed his belt and sword as quietly as he could manage, but the beautiful woman in his bed didn't stir.

They'd talk in the morning.

Maybe she'd even remember something about how she'd gotten to the beach. She'd said she'd gone to bed in a cottage not far from Dunvegan—but in her own century.

He stared down at her perfect form. Her thick flaxen locks were spread on his pillow as well as over her shoulder. She lay on her side, cuddled under his blankets. A thick MacLeod plaid lay on top, spread across Claire and the bed, and damn if he didn't like how the wool looked—on *her* in *his* bed.

Duncan's cock jumped. He paused with his hands

gathering up his plaid. He normally slept naked. He couldn't with Claire in his bed.

Why had he insisted she stay with him?

There were guest rooms at Dunvegan—hell, he could've had Janet put her in Alex's rooms, since their brother was gone.

The laird's quarters were the largest in the castle. His own were small in comparison, but more suited to him.

He shook his head at himself and dropped his plaid to the stone floor. Next was the leine. Duncan stood at the end of his bed nude.

Claire made a noise in her sleep and rolled over—toward him.

He gulped.

Duncan definitely wouldn't be crawling in his bed in his current state of undress.

"Trews. I need trews." If his bollocks were exposed much longer—to air or Claire's lovely sleep-warmed body, he had no ability to resist.

Sprinting to the trunk at the end of his bed, Duncan grumbled to himself in English and cursed in Gaelic.

She groaned.

He froze, only one leg inside the softest pair of breeches he'd managed to find. He never wore braies and didn't have any in his possession. Duncan could get some from the stores in the morning—or now. He hurried, stepping into the other pant leg, and yanking them up.

When the next noise the lass emitted sounded like a moan, his cock twitched. However, one glance at her face told him something was wrong.

Claire was tossing and turning in his bed, her fair brows knitted tight. Her skin had a slight sheen of sweat.

Duncan sat on the bed and reached for her.

Do not pull her into your arms. Just wake her.

"Lass?" He shook her shoulder gently, but she thrashed. "Claire-lass. Calm yerself."

She blinked as she came around, stilling beneath his fingertips. Her beautiful green eyes were heavy-lidded.

"Duncan?" Claire struggled to sit up, so he helped her, reluctantly forcing his hands to fall away when she leaned into his carved headboard.

"Are ye hale, Claire-lass?"

She wore the same chemise she'd donned after her bath. Even though the room was dim, he could make out her nipples, and see the impression of the darker skin surrounding them. Duncan swallowed a groan and tore his eyes away.

Perfect breasts he wanted to cup, knead, and taste. Swirl his tongue around…

Stop. Now.

"Still not a dream," she whispered.

Duncan quirked a half-smile, grateful for the distraction. He shifted on the bed. Hoped his trews wouldn't make his half-arousal obvious. "Nay. Yer here. Dunvegan Castle, Isle of Skye, in the Hebrides of Scotland."

"1672," they said the year at the same time.

Her shoulders drooped and his heart gave a funny patter. Duncan wanted to comfort her.

Keep your hands to yourself.

He chanted the order over and over.

Otherwise, he'd yank her to him, taste her mouth. Hold her. Then give all his attention to the glorious breasts he couldn't stop noticing. After that?

Take her.

Would she let him?

Duncan disregarded his desire and his notions.

No more dangerous thoughts.

He needed Claire's help to find his brother—provided she could remember anything about the Faery Stones. Then he'd help her get back to her time, as Duncan had promised her.

No use getting involved with her in any other way.

I'll get Alex back, and she'll leave.

"Duncan."

His eyes shot to her face when she said his name in a tone that made his bollocks ache. "Aye, lass?"

"I'm glad you found me."

"I'm glad I found ye, as well."

Silence descended, but it was no bother.

Duncan's hands itched to touch the soft skin of her cheeks.

"What am I going to do?" Her low voice was desperate, and his resolve cracked.

He scooted closer and cupped her face. Tilted upward so she had to look at him.

Do. Not. Kiss. Her.

"'Twill be well, Claire-lass."

Her expression softened and she wrapped her arms around his middle, burying her face against his bare chest.

Unmanly tremors chased each other down his spine as her warm breath caressed his skin, but Duncan couldn't push her away.

She needed comfort. He could do that. Even if it was going to take his self-control to the limits.

"Thanks, Duncan."

"Dinnae fash, lass." He contented himself by rubbing her back.

They didn't speak.

There was so much he wanted to tell her, plans they needed to make. Strategy to search for what he hadn't been able to find for the past six months.

No words formed in his mind to be born, his tongue was thick in his mouth.

Duncan just held the lass he'd found lost on the beach. Tried not to think about how satisfied he was with cradling a beautiful stranger.

Soon, Claire's breathing settled into a deep, even rhythm and a sense of *rightness* washed over him he promptly ignored.

He'd *never* held a lass while she slept, not even a former lover. When the rutting was done, he left, especially with the widow, Meg. She preferred he not even kiss her, so Duncan didn't.

She was a beautiful woman, so he wouldn't be opposed, but he respected her. When they came together it was for pure need on both their parts, but he made sure she was as physically sated as he was.

His heart might be content with his current state of innocence regarding Claire's nearness, but his cock certainly wasn't. Duncan was hard and throbbing, his arousal pushing against the fabric of his trews, but it wasn't the kind of friction he wanted.

He wanted to roll her over. Kiss her. Push her chemise up and off. Stare at her gorgeous curves before feasting on every inch of her body. He'd even light a new fire so he could see her.

Claire made a noise in her throat and nestled even closer. Her arm fell across his waist as if she owned him—and he didn't mind the idea. She rubbed her cheek on his chest.

Duncan swallowed a groan and his erection pulsed.

A little lower and her hand would rest much too close to his tender parts.

God's Blood, it's going to be a long night.

chapter seven

"I'm going with you."

A week had past and neither of them was closer to what they wanted.

Home for Claire and *Alex* for Duncan.

She still couldn't remember anything before "waking up" on the beach of Skye. Or how she'd gotten to his time. Even though he was convinced she'd traveled through the Faery Stones.

Duncan was supposed to leave in the morning to continue his quest for them. Stated he could delay no more, that he already had remained longer than planned.

Because of her.

The only thing that she'd accomplished, since arriving in the seventeenth century, was getting to know Duncan McLeod, which just resulted in her tug-of-war between her head and heart. Claire was having a hell of a time resisting him. She was drawn to him in a way she couldn't explain. A way that didn't make sense.

They'd spent their days together, talking of nothing but the Faery Stones, and where they could possibly be. They had even retraced her steps up and down the beach together multiple times, on foot and horseback. Of course, it hadn't gotten them anywhere.

Duncan laughed long and hard. "A lass on a pirate ship. 'Tis nay a pleasure cruise. I've told ye what I seek. We'll deign a 'nother way ye can help."

"Right." Claire took a deep breath. "Your purpose is *my* purpose. You want to find your brother, and I want to get home."

Did she?

Claire was already fond of this huge Highlander.

More than fond?

Her heart stuttered, but she ignored it. Duncan had been nothing but kind and honorable with her, even if his whole family — his whole clan — assumed she was sleeping with him.

Sleeping yes — as in getting rest in his bed.

Every night.

Sex?

Not so much.

God, I wish.

Duncan said nothing, but he stared at her like he always did.

Claire took a step toward him, closing the distance between them in his brother's office — ledger room — he'd called it. "We've talked about this. You need my help, and I *want* to help. Besides, maybe I can sense something, or something will jog my memory, and I can figure out how I got to that beach. It's worth a shot. So far nothing else has worked."

Duncan's massive chest rose and fell as he let out

an audible breath.

She was holding hers.

He was her *familiar* in this very foreign land of the past. She couldn't imagine being left in the castle while he was gone—for possibly months.

Claire adored his sister, liked his father, and of course little Angus, but...the thought of Duncan leaving her churned her stomach.

Historical romance novels hadn't covered just how difficult life in this time was. *Hard* work, and boring with no TV, movies, not even her damn MP3 player. What was worse, she couldn't read or speak Gaelic or Latin, so the books here were out, too.

No automation. *Everything* was manual labor, even cooking and laundry. Being a guest, she wasn't expected to help Janet and the female residents or servants, with the castle day-to-day, but she didn't want to sit around and be useless.

So, she'd been scrubbing floors on all fours, using a washboard to clean clothing and bed linens. Even smacking the dust out of tapestries.

Claire was a decent cook, so the previous night she'd helped in the kitchens, preparing a stew the men had seemed to enjoy, but she'd drawn the line at killing, even if she'd cooked and eaten the meat. Where she came from, beef and chicken came from the grocery store. That was how she'd always had to think of it or she probably wouldn't eat it. Seeing the rabbits before they'd been skinned, had been a little hard on her modern sensibilities.

The archaic defined roles of the genders were irritating but not a surprise.

On the other hand, the simplicity of life here appealed in a way that drew and shocked her, considering Claire was so plugged into her technology at home.

Smiles meant the same. Teasing, affection, and laughter were the same.

Love was the same.

She was getting used to wearing skirts, and corsets too, but she did miss underwear. Claire had worked so hard physically her body was sore, but it felt good. Like a hard workout in the gym. She felt kind of guilty because she'd begged Janet to have a bath daily and they didn't bathe every day in this time, but the lady of the castle had indulged her, probably because she was a guest. Claire couldn't quite transition to the idea of not bathing every day, especially after all the sweat she'd worked up from her new daily routine.

Duncan's people were kind and had welcomed her. Not even questioned her presence at Dunvegan, or in his rooms…in his bed.

"I see yer wisdom." He crossed his arms. "I dinnae like it. My men…are ruffians."

His thick brogue still made her heart beat harder.

The man was pure sex.

Claire took two more steps. She could feel the heat coming off his body, which felt so normal now, whenever she got close to him. Made her crave more. "You'll protect me." She wanted to inch even closer. If he reached for her, she could be in his arms in seconds.

A tremor shot down her spine.

"Will I now?" One corner of his mouth shot up. Amusement wrapped Duncan's words and her pulse kicked up another notch.

"Aye." She winked as she said his word.

Duncan smiled, and her stomach fluttered. "How 'tis that ye are so sure?" He bent his head low.

Claire gasped.

His lips hovered over hers.

Please, God. Let it happen finally.

Please kiss me.

"Because you're going to tell them I'm yours."

Duncan growled—honest to God growled.

Then his mouth crashed down on hers.

Claire moaned and moved into his chest, as well as into his kiss.

She should be embarrassed—even in her own head—that she'd been waiting for him to do this for a week now, but she wasn't. She just kissed him back.

He forced his tongue into her mouth, but she had no intention of fighting him.

Claire slanted her lips under his and kissed him harder, as Duncan wrapped his arms around her.

She'd not bothered with a chemise that morning, and the stupid wool of her skirt made her thighs itch as it brushed her skin.

His massive hands cupping her ass and lifting her scattered Claire's thoughts and she whimpered into Duncan's mouth.

He slammed his pelvis into hers and she melted, pushing right back.

God, she wanted him.

Burned for him.

Sleeping in his bed, but not in his arms, had left her with blue balls, especially the two nights he'd held her instead of avoiding contact.

Was it finally going to happen?

The Highlanders in her damn books never had as much control as Duncan MacLeod.

Unless he didn't want her — scratch that.

An erection was pressing into her stomach.

Claire rocked into him, kissing him even harder and squeezing her arms around his neck.

"Jesu, lass." Duncan tore away from her mouth, resting his forehead against hers. His hard chest pushed into her breasts as he panted. His high cheekbones were flushed with color, and the intense blue of his eyes, almost glowing.

One look at his handsome face, stole her breath all over again. He was so gorgeous. "Duncan, I want you," Claire confessed, unabashed.

He closed his eyes, groaning. "Dinnae be shy, are ye?"

"Do you want me to be?"

"Nay. I need ye, lass. My blood boils ta take ye."

"Then do it."

Duncan shook his head.

Claire flushed to her toes, cold despite his unwavering grip. Her heart plummeted to her stomach, and her temples throbbed. Pain washed over her.

She slipped out of his arms, fighting tears.

He's rejecting me?

Do not stand here and cry.

She should've known better than to admit how intensely she wanted him, even though it didn't make sense.

Of course, it only resulted in him crushing her.

It'd taken her years to work up her self-confidence with the opposite sex. Claire often covered things up with humor and brashness, something her sister said she did too much. It figured when it really counted, it bit her in the ass.

Only…why did she feel so much for a man she'd known a week?

She and Jules had grown up in foster care, so connections had always been something Claire had struggled with. Feeling one so intensely for Duncan after such a short amount of time was even more puzzling.

Perhaps something she didn't want to explore or define other than physically wanting him. She had most definitely wanted to explore that.

"Lass…"

Claire shook her head and averted her gaze.

"Forget it, Duncan."

His large, calloused hand swallowed hers and he whispered her name.

She choked back a sob, cursing herself for weakness and tears over something that shouldn't matter.

She *would not* cry in front of him.

Duncan squeezed her fingers and tugged.

Their gazes collided.

Claire gasped at the tenderness radiating from his eyes.

"I want ye, lass. Dinnae doubt it, e'er. I've ne'er wanted a woman like I want ye."

"Then…why?"

Duncan pulled her back to him, cupping her face. He pressed a light kiss to her lips.

Claire had to give a little smile; he was so gentle for a man his size.

The kiss was too quick.

She wanted more.

"I'll dinnae take ye, lass, 'til we're wed."

chapter eight

Claire's mouth opened and closed, but no words graced his ears. She blinked.

His stomach churned, but he gave her time to gather her thoughts. Duncan stared her down, watched her pale out. He grabbed her arm when she wavered on her feet.

Aye, she thinks you're mad.

Exactly *what* had just come out of his mouth?

Marriage?

With a woman not from his time?

A lass who had already made it clear she wanted to return to her own century.

Duncan had *promised* to help her in that quest, for Godssakes.

He'd proposed?

Aye.

He had to have her. Couldn't explain it, even in his own head.

Claire made his blood sing. Every night, she'd slept next to him since she'd arrived. Her sweet clean scent tickled his nose, made his cock ache.

Duncan had lain there, forcing his hands to remain at his sides, except for that first night he'd held her and the night before last when he'd been unable to resist doing so again.

She'd come into his arms, nestling against his chest without question both times.

He'd struggled to keep his hands to himself, keep his touch innocent.

The night before, Duncan had resorted to making himself lie facing the wall, instead of toward her. His self-control would've snapped otherwise.

It was all because of how Claire felt in his arms—one too many times. Her perfect softness against the hardness of his body.

She *fit* him and he was having a hell of a time resisting her.

Duncan burned to kiss her, take her. Over and over. Until she screamed his name and shattered in his arms.

He'd finally given into his fantasies and tasted her mouth.

When she'd proposed the farce of telling Riley O'Malley's crew she was his, Duncan couldn't resist the idea or her perfect delectable lips.

Claire's kiss had not disappointed, leaving his bollocks with a throbbing, heavy demand. Now he ached for her even more, but he couldn't give in.

He wouldn't touch her unless they were wed. Wouldn't risk having a bastard child. Couldn't stand the way people looked at his nephew with pity.

The poor lad wasn't even illegitimate. They just couldn't tell anyone the truth.

Yet, his brother always said. *Ever,* Duncan had always felt.

It didn't really matter.

Claire's going to leave as soon as you find the Faery Stones.

If she got with child, she'd take his blood away with her.

Nay.

He wouldn't let her go.

Duncan didn't think he could, regardless of a possible pregnancy. Couldn't explain why he was so drawn to the little blonde foundling from the future.

Claire didn't need to know *that* right now.

Would she still want to go if they wed?

She wanted him. Claire had made that plain.

"Marry you, Duncan?"

"Aye."

Her fair brows drew tight. "Why?"

A plan formulated in Duncan's mind, as he looked into her beautiful green eyes. "'Tis the only way."

She didn't need to know he was…embellishing.

"The only way for what?" Claire crossed her arms over her chest.

The movement made her breasts sit even higher in the corset, and he tore his gaze from there. Duncan was now familiar with what it felt like to have them flattened against him, as she wrapped herself around him, holding on tight, and returning his kiss with fervor.

'Twas worse than when he'd held her in his bed and kept his hands on her back, and *above* her waist.

"I dinnae be able ta bring ye aboard my ship, if we're no' wed."

"Why?"

"For your protection, lass."

Claire frowned. "So, you don't really *want* to marry me? Marriage in this time is forever, isn't it?"

Duncan wanted to marry her more than he'd ever wanted anything in his life. He seared for her.

Was it just about taking her?

He cleared his throat. "Aye, I do want ta wed ye, or I dinnae ask fer yer hand."

She looked even more confused, her sculpted eyebrows drawn tight and low. Then her eyes went misty, and Duncan ignored how his stomach jumped. "But Duncan, I need to get home. I have to leave. I *will* leave. You know that, right?"

He cupped her cheeks and drew her back to him. "Aye, I ken it."

"Then, why? Our marriage would be…temporary."

His mind rejected her statement, but he wasn't going to voice his disagreement.

Claire wouldn't marry him if he did.

"I need ta find my brother, as much as ye desire yer Texas. But I need to protect ye, if yer ta come with me. An' if I'm true ta ye, I want ye, lass. So, know this. If we wed, it shall be true; I'll have ye in my bed."

Claire smirked, and he had to order himself not to take her mouth again.

"I'm already in your bed, my laird." She looked at him dead-on, those green eyes glowing with desire again.

Her brashness made him want her even more.

Duncan growled. "Dinnae like I want ye ta be."

Crimson stained her cheeks. "I don't have to marry you to be with you. I want you."

"Nay without a wedding." He shook his head.

Claire frowned again. "Is it really for my protection, or is there more to this?"

His heartbeat stalled. The *more* was simply that Duncan wanted her. His men — Riley O'Malley's men — wouldn't touch her, with only a word from him.

He couldn't be completely honest because she'd never marry him.

Did he really want to marry a woman just to get inside her?

He probably should examine that, but his blood was still singing for her. Duncan just wanted her to say she would wed him.

Besides, what woman wanted to hear about a man's deepest fears?

Claire would see him as weak if he admitted that he feared physical desire would result in a child out of wedlock. His lack of self-control with her was bothersome enough.

Duncan didn't know if she wanted children. What

if the mention of her belly rounded with his bairn scared her into saying no?

Something that might not even happen at all?

"For yer protection, a'course."

She cocked her head to one side, and her flaxen locks danced over one shoulder. They were mussed from his hands, and he wanted to mess them even more. "They won't just believe you if you tell them I'm yours?"

"Aye, they would. But *marriage* 'tis the only thing 'twill keep you…untouched."

Claire shuddered. "On second thought, maybe I should stay here."

Coward.

You've already told her how badly you want her.

Stop being dishonest.

There wasn't a need to really scare her.

"If we wed, I'll have ye by my side," Duncan said.

Her eyes snapped to his face, and her breasts heaved with an audible breath. "Okay."

"Okay?" he repeated the odd word.

Over the week she'd been in his time, he'd gathered it meant some form of acquiescence. Claire used it diversely, but the more he spoke to her, the more he understood her speech patterns and choice of words.

"I'll marry you. If it's the only way."

His heart flipped and he couldn't hold back his grin. Duncan cupped her face. "Ye have ta want this, lass. We dinnae wed, if yer unwillin'."

Claire nodded but didn't dislodge his gentle hold. "I do. I want this. I want you, Duncan MacLeod."

He leaned down and sealed her *aye* with a kiss that melded into more.

By the time they parted, she was plastered to his chest and they both struggled for breath, panting hard, breasts against chest.

"'Tis settled. We wed on the morn. We'll tell my family an' have a priest summoned."

"So soon?" Claire swallowed.

Duncan had to force his eyes to hers, not kiss her throat like he wanted. If he gave in, the press of his lips on her neck would lead to more. He'd have to taste every inch of her.

He'd perch her on the edge of his brother's desk, push her skirt up, rip her leine off and *take* her in the bright afternoon light coming into the laird's ledger room.

Claire was his betrothed now.

Duncan's cock pulsed. He ignored it but pulled her closer instead of putting her away from him like he should. He needed physical space to clear his head. However, his limbs refused to adopt that notion.

"Aye. The ship 'tis already docked. I—we—must get back ta the quest."

"Okay." She didn't move out of his arms, but tremors racked her frame.

He rubbed her back, and Claire nestled closer,

resting her head against him and sighing.

Duncan kissed the crown of her fair head, ignoring the ache in his loins.

He had to marry her as quickly as possible.

Wouldn't survive another night with her in his bed and not be able to have her.

chapter nine

Claire watched the priest—who was really dressed like a friar, all in brown—wrap her and Duncan's joined hands in a thick strip of MacLeod plaid.

Her heart sped up.

I'm really doing this.

Marrying a man, she'd known for eight days. A man who was born over *three hundred* years before she was.

She'd dated older men before, but this took the cake.

Although Duncan was two and thirty—as he'd put it. Only five years older than Claire.

Still didn't absolve her from *crazy.*

She had to go home.

Back to Texas.

But for what?

Claire hated her job as an office manager for a small law firm. The only reason she'd stuck around was the pay was decent as well as the benefits. Her sister Juliette—Jules—was a cop, what Claire had always wanted to be, but had never had the guts to seriously pursue.

Her heart switched directions and gave a pang.

Jules. What about my sister?

Other than her sister, Claire had nothing and no one in the world she'd grown up in. They'd been raised in the Texas foster care system, from family to family, and not all of them had been great. They'd struggled to stay together, and Jules had always protected her. Always.

I told him this was temporary.

I have to go home.

She put worries about the future and her only blood relative out of her mind.

Claire looked up into Duncan's sapphire eyes. Her gut said she was making the right decision.

She'd still walk away if she ever managed to get home. He'd accepted that, so there were no worries.

She ignored the voice that asked, *do you want to?*

Could she live happily in the tail-end of the seventeenth century for the rest of her life?

What if I can't get home?

What if there's really no choice?

Those questions remained.

She was afraid of the answers.

Damn, she missed TV. Her laptop. Her stupid MP3 player.

Duncan had been looking for what he called the Faery Stones for half a year. He was convinced that was how Claire had ended up in 1672 on Skye.

What if they never found them?

All the more reason to marry him.

He wasn't wrong when he'd said she needed protection. Duncan was a Scottish nobleman. Even if he wasn't actually the laird, his family had means.

This land was truly wild compared to Claire's modern-day life.

She didn't want to contemplate what could've happened to her if Duncan, his father, and little Angus hadn't intended to fish that cold morning.

If she hadn't been able to get warm in his leine.

If someone with mal intent had found her naked...

Claire shivered and took a step closer to her soon-to-be husband.

"Are ye well, lass?" Duncan's whisper jolted her, but she smiled.

"Aye." She was getting used to the word, and loved the lopsided grin he always flashed when she said it. Maybe she'd be able to pull off that accent sooner than later, though she'd miss her Texas twang.

"Dinnae change yer mind?"

"No, my laird."

"Good." Duncan grinned and her stomach fluttered.

He actually wants to marry me.

God knows I want to get in his pants — err, under his kilt, but does he want me *for more than sex?*

The priest cleared his throat, as their conversation had interrupted him.

Duncan threw him a sheepish look and snapped

his mouth shut.

Claire couldn't stop staring at Duncan's lips. She wanted to kiss him again. Soon, she'd be able to, as his wife. Her heart missed a beat, and he squeezed her hands, as if he'd read her mind.

Logic reared its ugly head and reminded her that this was absolutely nuts.

She didn't want to resist the draw she had to this Highlander, and she was already standing beside Duncan MacLeod in front of a priest. It wasn't like she could back out now. Nor did she want to.

As crazy as that was — and it really was.

The monk-guy continued speaking to their small audience of Duncan's father, sister, and nephew, but Claire tuned them all out, staring up at the man she'd call husband in mere moments.

He stared right back, and she got lost in the blue of his eyes.

The strip of plaid fell away from their hands, and Duncan pushed a simple plain gold band onto her ring finger. Then he pulled her into his chest, wrapping his arms around her.

Claire reached to snake her arms around his neck and met his kiss. Their tongues twined and danced, duelled as he pressed deeper into her mouth. She moaned, her legs wobbling as desire swallowed her whole.

Duncan groaned and she felt his erection pushing into her stomach.

She wanted him.

Needed him.

Right. Now.

A deep throat cleared, and she jolted.

Her new husband pulled away. Color lit his high cheekbones and her heart stuttered.

Duncan had been as lost to the kiss as she was.

Her new father-in-law chuckled. "Save tha' fer later, lad."

Heat scorched her cheeks, and Claire buried her face against her husband's crisp white leine.

Duncan laughed but pinned her to his chest. "I need a minute, lass, or I'll embarrass myself," he whispered.

His warm breath above her ear shot a tremor down her spine.

He was still aroused and wearing a plaid, like normal.

She was torn between pride, since *she'd* done that to him, and even more embarrassment.

They were in a chapel.

Claire wanted to strip naked on command.

"Let us hie ta the great hall." Janet wore a grin. "Everaone's waiting. I've arranged a feast."

Claire heard the lively music, even before she entered the great hall on Duncan's arm.

Angus had already dashed inside.

Iain and Janet walked in front of them, and her new sister-in-law was giddy. Grinning from ear to ear and obviously proud of herself.

Claire gasped. Flowers were on every surface that would hold them. They were even wrapped around the great wood chandelier that hung above the tables.

Sweet scents mixed with roasted meat wafted through the large room.

So much for no fuss.

Janet had promised Claire she wouldn't make a big deal about things. Evidently, they had two different definitions.

All the MacLeods were already assembled to welcome the temporary laird and his new wife. Everyone was dressed in their best MacLeod-tartan attire and wore wide smiles.

Claire looked around at all the bright open expressions.

These people will hate me when I leave Duncan.

Her new husband squeezed her against his side as if he'd read her mind, then bent down to press a kiss to her cheek.

He wanted to marry me.

Duncan smiled, and Claire forced herself to return the gesture.

"Are ye well, lass?"

"I am, thanks. This place looks great."

Duncan's expression turned wry. "Aye, my sister

outdid herself. As usual."

"Obviously we need to further define *no fuss.*"

His smile slid into a grin that made her stomach somersault.

"Dinnae be likely she'd mind ye, any more than she's ever minded Alex or me, lass."

"Aye. 'Tis a weddin'. It must be celebrated," Janet said, beaming, as she stepped up behind them.

Duncan chuckled.

"I rest my case," Claire muttered, but she couldn't stop smiling.

Relax. You're married. To a dreamy hottie.

You get to have sex with him later.

Actual sex.

A tremor shot down her spine, and she shifted in her borrowed ladies' slippers.

"Let us feast," Duncan said, seating her at the head table.

"Then we dance!" Janet said brightly.

The evening was something out of a period-piece movie, but it was more wonderful than Claire could've ever imagined her wedding celebration to be.

The MacLeods were a lively bunch, full of laughter and love, and rowdiness when given *too much drink*—as Duncan put it.

She'd danced with his father, uncles, and a plethora of cousins, and even little Angus, until her feet were about to fall off.

When her husband claimed her for a dance and a

kiss, the catcalls made her face hot.

"Time ta retire, lass." His blue gaze darkened.

Claire didn't argue as she fell into his eyes. Her body warmed with only a look from him, and her limbs loosened, as she remembered how he'd kissed her when they'd been pronounced man and wife.

She yelped when Duncan swung her up over his shoulder like a ragdoll, but he just laughed and carried her from the great hall, as the men continued to throw ribald remarks at them.

Her cheeks burned and she was glad she couldn't see anyone as her up-do—courtesy of Janet—came undone and flew in her face.

Duncan kicked the door to his rooms shut after pounding up the stairs. He steadied her as he set her to her feet by the oversized bed, she'd shared with him for the past eight nights.

His gaze was intense as he looked down into her face. "Are ye innocent, lass?"

"Am I a virgin, you mean?"

"Aye."

"Oh, God no." Claire's neck seared when she processed the words she'd just blurted. "I mean, I'm not a slut, or anything."

"A...slut, lass?" Duncan was slow to repeat the obviously unfamiliar word.

She cringed. "Um...like a whore, but...she doesn't get paid."

Now his sapphire eyes were wide.

Dammit.

"A woman who likes a lot of sex," Claire said.

Oh. My. God.

Just tell him to give you a bigger shovel.

She threw her palms out. "Wait. No. I mean, I like sex, but…" More heat scorched her neck and cheeks, and she averted her gaze. Claire studied his room, trying to avoid the huge bed that dominated the left side.

The earthy scent of fresh peat drifted from the friendly fire burning in the big hearth.

Way to go with the new husband, Claire McGowan…or MacLeod.

Duncan's deep chuckle brought her head back around, and their eyes met. "I think I ken what ye mean, Claire-lass. We say, *loose with yer favors.*"

"Ah, yeah, that."

He studied her with that blue gaze, a mix of intensity and curiosity evident.

"Wait! That's not right, either. I'm not *loose with my favors.* I've had a few lovers, is all."

"E'er married?"

"No." She moved closer. "My time is different than yours."

"Marriage dinnae be sacred?" His dark brows drew tight.

"Well, I guess it is. I mean, to me it is. I…" Claire sighed. "Never mind. My words aren't cooperating."

Duncan cupped her cheeks. "The vows I made ta

ye, hold true fer me, lass. I belong ta ye. I hope tha same can be said a' ye."

Claire's heart sped into overdrive. He'd not spoken any words of love—or hell, even caring, but when he said things that flipped her stomach, she melted every time.

Even though the only thing he *had* told her was that he wanted her, she wanted to reassure him. "Of course. I meant it."

She did.

With all her…heart?

That's impossible.

Claire had only known him for eight days. Yet, she'd married Duncan MacLeod.

He smiled, and her thoughts scattered. When his lips hovered over hers, she closed the distance between their mouths, kissing him back with all her might.

Duncan rested his forehead against hers, when they parted, and a companionable silence descended.

"Are you upset that I'm not a virgin? Regret marrying me?"

"Nay."

"Are *you* a virgin?" Claire pulled back and arched an eyebrow.

There was no way a guy that looked like Duncan, kissed like Duncan, touched like Duncan, was an innocent virgin.

He had the nerve to chuckle. "Nay. Dinnae be such since I was a lad."

"Doncha think that's a little hypocritical?" She crossed her arms over her breasts and leaned even further away.

He smirked at her attempt at a Scottish accent. "I'm a man."

"And?" Irritation flared. Claire had to remind herself he was from the seventeenth century, not her own twenty-first. "I assume you weren't with other men?"

His eyes shot wide. "Jesu. Nay."

"Right. So, you ruined a few lasses, then?"

Duncan frowned. "Nay."

"So, you paid for it?"

His silence told her what she figured—and didn't want to know. "In my time, prostitution is illegal. And risky." Claire's voice dropped.

The idea of Duncan with other women—prostitutes to boot—burned in a way it shouldn't.

It wasn't like she had the right to be disappointed.

Her *claim* on him was brand new.

Thoughts like this make you *the hypocrite.*

You're not a virgin, neither is he. You're even.

Claire still didn't like it. She ignored her train of thought and focused on his words.

"I dinnae always *'pay fer it,'* as you say. But I won't lie ta ye, it's acceptable in my time. I've had a few lovers, as ye also put it."

"I don't like it, but I understand." She wanted to say so much more, but it wasn't happening.

Not when he looked at her like that.

Duncan cupped her face again.

His huge warm, calloused hands made her quiver, even though there was nothing sexual to the touch.

His eyes bored into hers again. "We come from different places, an' we both have a past, but we're here together now."

"Married." Claire smiled.

"Aye, good an' wed."

"So whatcha gonna do about it?"

Duncan growled, and her heart fluttered.

She met his kiss and slipped her tongue into his mouth.

chapter ten

Duncan buried his tongue in the lass' mouth. Damn, he couldn't get enough of his wife's taste. It was a mixture of mead she'd had at dinner and something that was just Claire.

Her sweet whimper was lost in the movement of their lips, but she kissed him back with the same fervor he offered her.

He tugged at the fancy fabric of the pale green wedding gown Janey and her seamstresses had made in two days' time. Duncan's plan of marrying Claire the morning after his proposal had been dismissed by his family. His sister had gotten her way and planned what she'd termed *a real wedding*.

The dress was bonnie, and first sight of his lass from the far future in it, walking down the small aisle of the chapel had stilled his heart, but if he didn't get it *off* her, Duncan was going to rip it off.

"Duncan, don't tear my dress," Claire chided, as if she'd read his mind. She took a step back and started to unlace the front of the corset.

It was shimmery and low-cut, displaying enough cleavage to make him growl all evening—any time one of his kinsmen had the bollocks to look her way.

However, being laced up the front would have her spilling into his hands sooner.

Smirking, Duncan took the ribbon from her hand and deftly undid it. Every inch of skin he exposed made his cock harder.

He remembered her perfect breasts from the day they'd met on the beach. Then the mere impression of them every night in his bed. His hands itched to cup and knead. His tongue burned to tease her nipples, feel them harden against his lips.

"Claire-lass," he groaned.

She batted his hands away when he reached for her. Claire wiggled, and the bodice of the dress fell, revealing a chemise that did nothing to hide her body from him. It was much fancier than the one she normally slept in, covered in lace. The fabric had a sheen to it as well.

He didn't care.

Duncan wanted it *off.*

His cock kicked against the material of his plaid, but still his woman wouldn't let him touch her, sliding back a step when he reached for her.

"Patience, husband."

He growled and shot forward, gripping her face, and crashing his lips into hers. Duncan kissed her until she wavered on her feet, clinging to the linen of his tunic with tight fists.

"Not fair," Claire panted into his mouth.

"I've wanted ye from tha moment I saw ye on tha

beach. I've been *patient.*"

Her breasts rose and fell against him, and he burned to see her completely bare.

"Take the gown off," he ordered.

A smile played at his bride's lips as she regained her composure. "You have clothing to lose, too, you know."

Words of retort dissolved as Claire pushed the dress downward. It gathered at her waist, then she shimmied her hips, and it pooled at her feet on the stone floor with the barest rustle.

His room was alight with candles in every corner—thanks to his sister. Claire's body was surrounded by the soft glow like a radiant aura.

Duncan's breath caught in his throat. The diaphanous fabric of the chemise held no secrets, but his wife looked like an angel. It mattered not he'd seen her naked. The way she was now was more beautiful than ever before.

She reached up, letting her flaxen locks loose from the elaborate style Janet had done up for their wedding. Her hair cascaded around her shoulders, and she flashed a smile, enhancing his enchantment with her.

"Claire-lass." His tongue was thick, his mouth dry.

He *scorched* for her.

"Duncan." Claire's whisper made his heart thunder and his erection pound.

"Come here."

She didn't hesitate as she stepped to him.

Duncan kissed her again, but this time it was a soft thing with no demand. He trailed his lips down her neck, nibbled her earlobe, then pushed the lace of her sleeve off her shoulder to kiss her collar bone.

Claire moaned, her hands flexing on his forearms. "I want you."

"The feeling 'tis mutual, lass." His voice had gone thick on him, barely recognizable to his own ears.

"Get naked for me, Duncan. Please. I want to see you. I want to touch you. I want to get into that big bed and have my way with you."

He chuckled and brushed two fingers down her cheek. "Yer way wit' me, ye say?"

She grinned and nodded, pressing a kiss to his palm.

Her beautiful pale skin was flushed pink, and he wanted to make her that particular color over her whole body. She already looked ravished, and he'd hardly gotten started.

A shiver went straight to his cock. "I s'ppose I dinnae deny my Lady MacLeod."

She paused. "I am, aren't I?"

"What, Claire?"

"Lady MacLeod."

"Aye, yer my wife. *My* Lady MacLeod. Until Alex returns, yer *the* Lady of the Clan."

Claire's pretty visage sobered. "No pressure."

Duncan stroked her high cheekbones with his thumbs. "Nothin' yer nay capable of. Dinnae fash o'ermuch."

"What do I know about being a Scottish noblewoman?" she whispered.

He dipped his head down to taste her again, and Claire kissed him back without hesitation. When they parted, Duncan rested his forehead against hers. "'Tis our wedding night. Let us leave worries lie."

"You're right. Get naked, husband."

He grinned, releasing her, and whipping his leine up and off. "Ye as well, wife."

Claire's green stare seared him, as she removed her chemise. She gasped as Duncan let his plaid hit the stone floor. Her eyes moved up and down his frame.

His cock jutted, as if it needed to show off.

A groan fell from his mouth when she licked her lips.

"Damn," she muttered. She made no move to cover her nudity.

He frowned. "Damn? Somethin' wrong?"

"No." Her blonde locks shifted as she shook her head. "You're…just…wow."

Duncan smirked. "'Tis good?"

"*Very* good." Claire dragged her hands over the hard muscles of his chest, tracing his abdominals until they jumped.

His nipples ached, his skin warmed and burned every inch her fingertips caressed. Duncan ordered himself not to squirm and ignored the demand between his legs.

When she encircled him with her hand, he cried out—couldn't have held it in if he'd tried. "Dinnae be shy," he panted the words.

"Why should I be? You've told me you belong to me, right? I'm going to enjoy you." Her voice was confident, but her cheeks were pink, and the appeal made his blood boil.

Claire was an intriguing mixture of sultry and innocent, and he had to have her *now*.

Duncan swept her up into his arms.

They both gasped when their naked skin came together, but he didn't stop, covering her mouth with his and carrying her to his bed.

Finally, her presence in it would no longer be torture. He'd have her, take her as many times as he wanted.

Claire *belonged* to him.

She wanted him as much as he wanted her, and that made Duncan's need surge.

He put her at the center of his bed and followed her down, settling in the cradle of her body and deepening their kiss.

Claire was still right with him, twisting her tongue around his, exploring his mouth as he plundered hers.

His wife wove her fingers in his long hair, pulling as she moved closer into his chest, but Duncan didn't care.

He split her thighs with a knee, pushing a hand between them and caressing the curls that guarded her core.

She gasped into his mouth but lifted her hips into his touch. "Duncan…"

"Jesu, lass. Yer wet…" he teased the bundle of nerves at the top of her sex.

Claire whimpered and her head fell back into his pillows as he further explored her slick folds.

Duncan pressed a row of kisses down her slender throat. His erection was trapped pleasantly between them, but the friction wasn't enough.

When his bollocks tightened like he was about to lose it, he sucked in air and lifted his head to meet the heavy-lidded emerald eyes of his bride. "I want ta worship yer body, lass, but now…"

"I know. You're killing me. Duncan, just get inside me."

He crushed his eyes shut, as she writhed beneath him, rubbing his cock.

Urgency boiled his blood. Duncan pressed a hard fast kiss to Claire's mouth and grunted when her nails bit into the skin of his shoulders.

"Duncan…"

His name was a plea he couldn't refuse.

He would taste her all over, but it would have to be later, after he'd made her his. If he waited, he was likely to lose his seed all over her belly without ever joining their bodies. Like an overtaxed virgin.

Duncan gripped his cock and guided himself to her glistening swollen flesh. One look at her pink sex made him groan. He sank his teeth into his bottom lip and prayed for control.

Claire might not be innocent, but he still wouldn't take her roughly. Would never hurt her, despite how great his need to fill her, feel her to his bones.

He pushed forward, entering her body slowly inch by inch, until they were one. Duncan filled her to the hilt.

She closed her eyes, moaning his name and wiggling beneath him.

"Lass," he grunted. "Yer tight. Yer…"

"Yours, Duncan MacLeod." She tugged him down, forcing her tongue into his mouth.

He let her control things, then he started to thrust. "Mine." Duncan shoved the word into her mouth, and she pushed her lips into his, demanding yet another kiss.

Claire met his next stroke, and the one after that, tilting her hips to take him deeper and wrapping her legs around his waist.

They fell into a frantic rhythm, his wife matching his every kiss, every touch.

She was flushed pink from head to toe. Her skin glowed from the color that he had burned to see.

Duncan was lost, enchanted by her.

The scent of her damp skin. The feel of her hands on his sweaty back, and her lips on his neck.

He'd never had a more responsive lover.

When her inner muscles clutched at his sex,

tremors chased each other down his spine. His bollocks shook as he surged into her one more time.

Claire threw her head back and called his name, eyes closed and her body stiff beneath his as climax hit them both.

He grunted, and his erection kicked inside her, his release going deep. Her body milked his, pleasure hit him in waves. His muscles went lax, and he fell onto her, but she held him tight, whispering his name over and over.

Duncan fused their mouths, and the kiss melted into something languorous. Deep, meaningful.

Words of affection—maybe more—played on the tip of his tongue.

How had he survived before this woman?

Her breasts pushed into his chest as she panted.

Duncan's breathing was just as rough. His mind spun.

Chaos.

He'd rutted many a lass—as he'd told Claire. His brother had often accused him of being too loose with his favors. It was probably true, maybe even embarrassingly so. He'd been with the widow Meg more times than he could count.

None of his previous lovers had scrambled him like the lass currently in his arms.

Duncan had just *made love* for the first time in his life.

He gripped her upper arms and flipped them.

Claire landed on his torso, as his softening cock slipped from her body, and his bride snuggled into his chest.

He was at a loss for words. He wrapped his arms around her.

Could he tell her what was racing through his head?

Nay.

She'd think his feelings were as crazy as his sudden marriage proposal had been.

Although Claire *had* married him.

"Mine." The word fell from his lips.

The smile that bloomed made Duncan's heart stutter. "Mine, too." Claire traced one of his nipples with her index finger and an unmanly shiver racked his frame.

"Lass, that was—" Words failed, and her cheeks pinked again when their gazes collided.

Claire pressed her lips to his. "Perfect."

Duncan reached up, needing to touch her face, and staring. He still couldn't form a damn sentence.

Her expression was soft. Her beautiful green eyes were hazy and heavy-lidded. Her face was still crimson, her lips swollen from his and her hair pleasantly mussed.

He'd never seen a more alluring lass in his life.

When she yawned, he chuckled.

"Sorry," she muttered. "Long day, I guess."

Smiling, Duncan hauled her closer, but she nestled

into him without hesitation. "Finally."

"Finally?"

"Yer in my bed as ye should be. In my arms."

She flashed a sleepy smile. "No place I'd rather be."

Duncan mulled over her words, as Claire's breathing fell into the deep, even rhythm he was used to hearing now after more than a week.

The lass had married him with the understanding it was for her protection. She would still return to her time when he found the Faery Stones. He'd promised he would help her.

Acknowledged that their marriage was temporary.

He ordered himself not to think on it too much.

Duncan already couldn't stand the idea of letting her go.

chapter eleven

The red taxi drove down the long-pebbled roadway, jarring Claire with the uneven surface. However, the sight before her quickly caught her attention, as the eight-hundred-year-old Clan MacLeod stronghold loomed.

Dunvegan Castle.

She gasped. "It's gorgeous."

Her Scottish cabby chuckled, tipping his cap over his too-long red locks. "As I understand it, Laird MacLeod is away on business. I know the caretaker. He'll show you around, an' I'll be back for you this afternoon."

"Thank you. I really appreciate this. I'm so glad I get to see it."

"Not a problem, lass."

Claire smiled and got out of the small car. She probably shouldn't have ditched her tour group, but for an up-close-and-personal look at Dunvegan Castle—well, it'd be worth the "we were supposed to stay together" scolding she'd get from the grumpy guide.

A groan made her open her eyes. "A dream?"

She sat up, swallowing a wide yawn and looked around. A fireplace across a large room jarred her.

"Claire-lass?" The moment she heard his voice, the last week, and a half—the last three nights—came rushing back.

Married.

Duncan.

Best sex of her life. In his arms; in his bed.

Claire gasped.

Duncan sat up next to her, his dark brow furrowed. He reached for her. "Claire?"

"I remember!"

Her new husband cupped her face and studied her. His blue eyes scorched even in the dimness of the room. "Remember?"

"How I got to Skye, in my time."

"Aye?"

"I…I was on vacation—visiting. Taking a break. I snuck away from my group to have a private tour of Dunvegan."

Duncan smirked. "Dunvegan? Glad ta hear our home still stands in yer time."

Our home.

Oh my God.

Claire cleared her throat and nodded. "It's as gorgeous as ever." She racked her brain for more, but nothing would come. She'd gotten the sense she was staying on the isle, but surely not *at* Dunvegan.

Maybe a hostel or a bed and breakfast?

"I can't believe it," she breathed.

"What, Claire-lass?"

"I actually saved up enough money to come to Scotland. It was always my dream."

Duncan's expression was thoughtful. "Yer here, aye."

"Well, I never dreamed I'd come back in time, though I've dreamt about many a hot Highlander."

Claire had explained that she'd always been obsessed with his era and read many fictional stories — romance novels.

Whenever she spoke of the future, he'd listen quietly as his mind processed things he'd never fathomed. She tried to keep it simple — but honest.

As intrigued as he was, he didn't seem to want to see modern times. He was content with where he belonged.

Duncan growled, and her belly flipped. "Do I fit yer desires?"

"Aye, my laird." Claire shivered as his gaze devoured her.

He grabbed her up, flipped them and pressed her down into his oversized bed. Duncan fused their mouths, forcing his tongue inside and swallowing her moan.

"We should sleep." She pressed the words into his lips. "We have a big day tomorrow."

They were to depart in mere hours.

To continue Duncan's quest for the Faery Stones.

"My need of ye is greater than my need fer sleep."

Claire whimpered as her husband's hand

skimmed her lower belly. Her sex throbbed, begging for his touch.

It didn't matter how often he'd touched her. He'd been inside her so many times she'd lost count in the three days since they'd exchanged vows. Her body was sore, but she'd never tell him *no*.

She ached for him in a way she never had for any other man. Claire would never get enough of Duncan MacLeod.

The lack of condoms and the fact she'd left her birth control pills in the future should be more concerning than it was. The idea of getting pregnant by Duncan excited her, not worried her.

She'd called herself foolish when the thought had first crossed her mind, but memories of Texas faded when she was in her husband's arms.

Claire moaned as his stubble brushed the soft skin above her sex.

When he parted her thighs with huge, calloused hands, she sighed.

Her body relaxed into the bed.

She buried her hands in his long dark hair and sucked in a breath when she felt his tongue on her clit. Her heart kicked up a notch and she cried out when Duncan sucked her into his mouth.

"Jesu, Claire-lass. The way ye taste…I need more." His words vibrated against her sensitive skin and tremors racked her frame as pleasure threatened to swallow her whole.

Duncan slipped one finger inside her, then another. He found a rhythm with hand and mouth and her pulse thundered in her ears as pressure melded with physical feeling; climax started to build.

It was just as intense as their lovemaking, but this lacked urgency. He was making *her* feel good.

A steady rise of waves flowing over her body, sucking her down and pushing her up until the wall broke, cascading over the edge like a waterfall.

Claire cried out, tugging his hair. Her whole body stiffened. Orgasm roared and her inner muscles tensed.

Then he was there, pulling her into his arms, filling her sex with his, kissing her mouth before she could even take a breath.

She wrapped her arms around his neck, rubbing her tongue against his, moaning at the mix of her essence with Duncan's familiar taste.

He surged forward.

Claire met his thrust without pause or conscious thought. Had to get closer to him. Merge her form into his. Her limbs were heavy, her skin overheated and sweaty, but she needed *more*.

She pressed her breasts flat to his chest, moving with him, under him, until their bodies had no rhythm. They both took and gave, answering each other's demands with grunts, moans, and groans.

Her whole body was on fire for him. Every touch, every kiss, even every stroke threatened to make her combust from the inside out, despite the orgasm he'd given her before pushing inside her.

"Lass," he breathed into her neck, burying his face against her. Duncan kissed the spot, and his back stiffened. One last pump and he whispered her name as he came inside her, squeezing her in his arms.

His orgasm triggered hers; Claire cried out. Her thighs shook and her core throbbed as her hips rocked of their own accord. She had to pant to breathe, her head spinning when her vision finally started to clear.

Duncan collapsed on top of her, but she held him tight, reveling in his weight like always. He was so big, but he'd never hurt her, despite the size of his frame.

Claire loved to snuggle into his chest after they made love. Study the contrast of his darker tanned skin against hers. Look at their legs entwined.

She'd never considered herself overly feminine, but seeing her slender thighs and knees between his muscular ones made her feel girly.

The way he always ran his hands down her naked body as he held her made her feel protected and cherished.

Loved?

Claire's heart pounded as she looked into her husband's face.

Duncan had his eyes closed. His high cheekbones were flushed with color. Rough stubble made her want to drag her fingertips through it and trace his kiss-swollen lips. His dark hair was mussed. She wanted to smooth it out and mess it up even more at the same time.

She'd done that too him.

Given him pleasure.

Made this big strong warrior look so peaceful.

Sated.

Lifting her head, Claire pressed her lips to his in a tender kiss he didn't hesitate to return or deepen.

Duncan kissed her until her head swirled with confusion and unwanted feelings.

I'm falling for him.

Hard. Fast.

After twelve days?

Hell, yes.

Sex with previous lovers had never felt like it did with Duncan. Even good sex.

This was more.

This was making love.

Emotion threatened to bowl her over.

How can I leave him?

How could she walk away from Duncan MacLeod if — when — they found the Faery Stones?

How can you stay in the foreign land of 1672?

Besides, Duncan had never told her how he felt about her. *If* he felt anything for her other than lust.

Claire crushed her eyes shut, breaking their kiss, and burying her head against his shoulder.

"Claire-lass? Somethin' wrong?" Duncan shifted, slipping from her body, and rolling to his back. He took her with him, and she nestled into his side like always.

Like we fit together.

Natural.

Right.

Her bottom lip trembled. She couldn't look at him.

Duncan cupped her cheeks and tilted up. "Claire?"

She forced her mouth to curve and met his gaze. Swallowed against the sudden lump in her throat, at the tenderness she read in those sapphire eyes. "I'm good. You…make me feel awesome."

He smiled and kissed her mouth. It was sweet and gentle and made her stomach flutter.

"Ye do the same fer me."

"Duncan…" Claire shook her head, as words dissipated.

What was she supposed to say?

Demand the *right* words from him?

What *she* needed to hear didn't mean it was what *he* felt.

Should Claire admit feelings that scared the hell out of her, because she was still planning on walking away?

"Aye, lass?" His thumbs made lazy strokes on her cheeks.

His touch, so perfect, made her feel worse. For a big tough guy, Duncan was the most giving, selfless lover she'd ever had. He cared about *her* pleasure and loved making her feel good.

When he told her, it seared her face, but he *showed* her even more often than he explained it.

Does that mean he cares for me?

"No one's ever made me feel like you do." The words were out of her mouth before Claire could censor them.

Way to go, blurt-girl.

His slow smile warmed her heart and her limbs.

Duncan kissed her long and thoroughly, making her already satiated body boneless.

"'Tis the same fer me, Claire-lass." The whisper was pressed into her mouth; his statement distorted.

Claire understood every word—and clung to it.

chapter twelve

laire gaped. It was a freaking *pirate* ship. She tightened her grip on her husband's arm.

"Lass?" Duncan's blue eyes held concern, and he pulled her to his side.

"Your ship…" she stared up at the tattered black flag.

Yes, black.

Like right out of the *Pirates of the Caribbean* movies, except the boat had the name *the Fancy Seer* in gold lettering on the wide back.

"Well, 'tis a borrowed vessel ta be true." Duncan whispered the words right above her ear, which only made her heart pound at his nearness.

Her body lit up from the inside out, as always for the man she called husband. "It's a pirate ship." Claire's voice dropped on the word *pirate* and Duncan smirked.

"Right." He nodded, as he used the word she said so often, the way she said it. "I explained that ta ye."

"I didn't take you literally."

He smirked. "Ye should've."

"I see that." Her mouth was dry. Her fingers flexed on his thick forearm. "Maybe I *should* stay on Skye."

"Oh, nay. Ye've made yer bed, Claire-lass. I'll have

ye by my side."

She groaned. "I've made *your* bed, you mean."

Duncan dragged two fingers down her cheek. "Complainin'?" His confident tone made heat creep up her neck. He bent down, lips hovering above her ear again. "I like when ye scream my name, *mò gradh*."

"*Mò gradh*. Claire struggled to repeat the Gaelic words. "What does that mean?"

He flashed a grin and kissed her.

She leaned into him, and Duncan held her tight as she moved her mouth under his.

Desire unfurled low and hot, and her sex throbbed. She was going to have to start thinking of herself as the women did in her books when they wanted to chide themselves.

Wanton.

Because no matter how many times she'd been with Duncan, he turned her on *completely* with just one kiss.

Claire squeezed her thighs together, but it did nothing for the empty ache between her legs.

"Now, now, my laird," a male voice drawled.

The accent wasn't Scottish, it was Irish.

She pulled away from her husband. Made eye-contact with a man about her height.

He had long red hair, bound tight at the back of his neck, and creepy pale blue eyes. His face was riddled with pock marks.

The pirate wore a light beard and a smirk that shot

a tremor down her spine. He wasn't ugly, but he was definitely rough around the edges, and looking the part of what he was.

He made her skin crawl.

Claire shifted closer to Duncan, as the redheaded man made no secret of appraising her body, his eyes trailing her frame.

She regretted the leather trews—as Duncan had called the pants she wore. At least in a skirt the bastard couldn't have looked at her legs. Of course, pants were more her style—even if they were far from her favorite jeans.

She shivered.

The pirate's gaze burned, but not in a good way. More like she was a meal to be devoured.

Duncan growled, but he shot his hand out for a shake. "Riley O'Malley."

Riley's smirk deepened. He didn't accept her husband's shake but bowed at the waist.

Claire frowned.

The jerk was mocking her man.

"My laird. Milady."

Duncan was stiff as he looked down at the pirate. Not like he was openly demeaning the man or anything, although he should be. Her husband just towered over the pirate.

"This is my wife. Ye shall refer ta her as 'Lady MacLeod' and nothin' less. Order tha men ta keep their eyes in their heads an' hands ta themselves—or *I'll* deal wit' them wit' my sword. *Yer* included in that." His voice was harder than she'd ever heard it, and Claire quivered at his side.

"My men are yers ta *direct*, Captain." Riley winked at her, even though he addressed Duncan.

She wanted to hide behind her husband. This pirate dude seriously gave her the heebie jeebies.

Claire looked around the cave. It was a wonder the ship fit inside, even with all the rocky width, but she understood the need to hide the vessel after seeing it.

Duncan's father slowly rowed away in the birlinn they'd arrived in. It was a speck compared to *the Fancy Seer*, but it was a boat her husband had said he was comfortable in.

Seeing him on the sea was an eye-opener. He seemed to sense the water as he navigated through it.

Her husband was a natural born sailor.

Before they'd departed, he'd stood at the end of the birlinn — what Claire would've called a skiff — the wind in his hair, head tilted back, eyes closed.

Sexy as hell.

Her body had heated just watching him in his element. That had been even before she'd seen the play of his muscles when he'd helped his father row.

Iain MacLeod was the only one who knew of their destination. The rest of the MacLeods assumed he was off on Clan business.

All they knew of Alex was that he was away as well — no one except for Janet, Iain and Angus knew he was in the hands of the Fae, life endangered.

"Welcome aboard, Lady MacLeod. I'm first mate ta yer man." Riley O'Malley flashed a smile that made her gut churn.

This jerk was a control freak, letting Duncan be captain only because there was something in it for him.

Claire wanted to kick him in the balls.

Why did her husband feel it was necessary to employ pirates?

Couldn't he find the Stones without them, but with *her* help?

Was this Bridei-seer just *that* good?

No way, or it wouldn't have already been six months.

Claire forced a polite nod and slipped her arm into Duncan's.

Her husband pulled her to his side and patted her knuckles.

As soon as they'd boarded *the Fancy Seer*, a dark beauty slid forward. She was clad in long black skirts, with a bright red sash around her waist.

Her midnight corset was so tight Claire was afraid if the woman bent over her knockers would fall out. No tunic beneath her bodice. So, the display of her body was on purpose.

She offered a coy smile for Duncan and openly flirted with him, as if Claire didn't stand next to him, her arm tucked into his elbow.

Claire narrowed her eyes and held her tongue because her husband didn't respond.

Duncan batted the woman's hand away when she attempted to drag her fingers down the front of his shirt.

Somehow, Claire didn't think it was merely for her benefit.

He seemed just as disgusted by the woman and her attempted ministrations as she was, if his tight jaw was any indication.

"This is Bridei, she's the seer," her husband said. "When we get close, she says she can sense the Faery Stones and open the doorway into the Fae Realm."

The woman's dark eyes finally settled on Claire. One ebony eyebrow shot up and she put her hand to her bosom like she was surprised. Like she hadn't noticed Claire before.

Who the hell does this bitch think she is?

Claire swallowed a scowl.

She was so irritated and didn't even focus on Duncan's words. Otherwise, she might've been fascinated with a real seer.

"Good day, milady." The woman offered a bow like the pirate captain had, but then she did a double take on Claire, her eyes raking her frame. The seer swayed on her feet, her olive complexion paling, her mouth half-agape.

Riley grabbed her arm to keep her on her feet, evidently. "Bridei?"

"Riley. Riley. The lass."

"Me?" Claire asked.

The pirate and the seer ignored her.

She exchanged a glance with her husband.

Duncan returned his stare to Riley and Bridei, his mouth a hard line.

"Excuse us, my laird. I must speak with Riley in private." The woman grabbed the pirate captain's arm, and they practically ran around the corner to get away from them.

Duncan watched them go, but Claire tugged on his forearm. He'd dropped her hand and had his arms crossed over his broad chest.

"Was she talking about me? Am I *the lass*? What the heck happened?"

His blue gaze settled on her. "I dinnae ken, *mò gradh*. But I intend ta find out." Duncan caressed her cheek, then strode after Riley and his seer.

Claire looked around the wide deck.

Men bustled, yelling to each other as they readied the ship for departure.

A real freakin' pirate ship.

Everything looked tattered.

What if they sank?

Claire shook her head. It was dim in the cave, but light came in from the wide mouth, as well as from somewhere above them. Obviously, there was a hole in the "roof."

An old guy flashed a toothless grin, and she shivered.

She looked in the direction her husband had gone

and rubbed her arm. He was out of sight now, and her heart skipped a beat. "Hey, wait for me!"

chapter thirteen

The low whisper caught his attention when he heard his wife's name.

Bridei had her head bent tight to her lover, the mixture of red and black hair obscuring their faces.

They'd beat him to the captain's cabin, standing not far from the bed Duncan was supposed to share with Claire.

He'd never witnessed the seer react like she had when she'd seen his wife.

Why so secretive with the pirate captain now?

Bridei had been shaking from head to foot.

Her dark eyes went wide when she saw him striding toward them. Her olive skin—denoting her gypsy heritage—had gone even paler than when they'd been on deck. "My…my…laird."

"Captain." Duncan locked his jaw.

"Aye, sorry my—Captain."

"What's wrong?" he demanded.

Riley straightened, glaring right back. "Watch yer tone with my woman." However, he, too, was pale.

Ice raced down Duncan's spine. "Tell me what's goin' on. Now."

"Yer woman. We know her," Bridei confessed.

Protective instincts flared and Duncan bit down

until pain shot into his gums. "Know her?"

"I…think…I brought her here."

Brought her here?

She couldn't know Claire was from the future…could she?

How?

Unless her words were true…

Duncan growled, making his fist tighter with each word that fell from the seer's lips. His da hadn't raised him to strike a lass, but he was tempted. "*My* lass—"

"Is not from our time." Bridei's voice dropped.

He fought a tremor. Ordered himself not to show a reaction. Couldn't appear weak in front of the pirate captain.

Or put his wife's life in danger.

What would they want from her if he confirmed what they seemed to know?

"The Faery Stones," the seer breathed.

Duncan glared. "Where are they?"

The gypsy woman paled even further and backed into the wall of the cabin.

The pirate and his lover exchanged a look and said nothing.

Duncan stalked forward. His hand itched to draw his sword. He sucked in a breath and towered over Riley and Bridei. "*Where* are the Faery Stones?"

"Not far." The seer's voice quaked.

"What do ye mean, *not far*?" he bit out.

"They're here. On Skye." Her voice was small, and

she cowered, but he tore his eyes away from her.

"Ye *lied* ta me. Found the Stones in secret. Ye had *no* intention a' revealin' their location." He snatched Riley by the collar of his leine with both fists. "Ye greedy, bastard."

"We didn't lie!" Bridei tugged on his forearm.

Duncan knocked her away, lifting the slimy pirate and shoving him into the wall of the captain's cabin.

Breath whispered out of Riley's mouth, and his cheeks became as red as his hair with every ounce of pressure Duncan applied. He gurgled and struggled, but the smaller man didn't have a chance against his strength.

The pirate's filthy blunt nails bit into his hands as Riley fought him, but Duncan didn't loosen his grip. His feet dangled off the planked floor, and he tried to wiggle his shoulders to no avail.

"Duncan, stop. You're going to kill him."

His wife's voice from the doorway gave him pause, but he didn't release Riley O'Malley.

"'Twas the idea," he grunted.

"Let him down so he can explain." Only Claire's soft hand on his arm made his hand let go. "How do they think they know me?"

Claire heard all that?

She must've been standing there for a while.

Duncan took a step back and Riley O'Malley slid to the wood floor coughing.

The pirate made it to his feet but doubled over to

catch his breath.

The seer remained frozen and stared at Claire, a few feet from them. "Ye…ye are alive."

"Why wouldn't I be?" His wife's fair brow was furrowed, and she reached for him. She entwined their fingers and Duncan let her, hauling Claire closer to him.

No matter what was about to happen, he'd protect her. With his life, if it was required.

"We left ye…"

"Left her where?" Duncan growled.

"Bridei, not another word." Riley regained his composure, but his face was still red. He slipped in front of his woman and glared.

"She'll tell all, or I'll hie ye ta the wall again, but this time I *will* kill ye."

The pirate captain squared his shoulders, but he couldn't hide his blanch. "We'll tell ye nothin' without more gold."

Duncan took a step forward, snarling. "I will kill ye. Now."

"Duncan." Claire's voice was calm.

It startled him, but both Riley and Bridei looked at his wife.

"I remember."

"Remember what, *mò gradh*?" His voice was gentle

as Duncan turned to her. Much different than it had been moments before when he'd threatened the pirate.

When Bridei had said something about leaving her, tremors had racked Claire's frame until her teeth rattled.

"I was running on the beach."

The seer whimpered, but Duncan put a large palm up.

Claire looked at the redheaded pirate, then Bridei. Sucked in a breath as everything came back. Rushing into her head with too much speed. Like a movie on fast forward, she could see the picture in her head but didn't understand everything.

Dizzy.

Must have swayed, because Duncan grabbed her arm, pulling her closer.

"Aye, *mò gradh.* Ye were running by the water before I found ye."

Claire shook her head. "That's not what I mean. I was staying at a cottage on Skye. In my time. I woke at six and decided to run on the beach before meeting my tour group for breakfast. It was the day after the caretaker of Dunvegan took me on a tour. I had my headphones in, listening to music."

The pirate and his girlfriend looked confused, heads cocked to one side, furrowed brows as they listened, but Duncan understood her words. She'd explained what an MP3 player did.

Three sets of eyes stared as Claire tried to make

sense of the memories. "I heard…this popping sound. Over and over, getting louder and louder. I thought something was wrong with my MP3 player, but the beach got windy. I looked around, but there was no change in the water. I'd thought it was really weird—sudden—but I grabbed my MP3 player from where it was clipped on my waistband. Right when I stared at the screen, there was this *loud* tear, like the sound of ripping paper. The wind threw me forward. My head spun. I think I passed out."

"Ye came back in time." Duncan caressed her cheek, then glared at Riley and Bridei.

The seer stood behind the protection of her boyfriend, peeking over his shoulder like a little kid.

"That's all I remember. I need her." Claire pointed, "to fill in the blanks. What'd you mean, you left me?"

"Ye came through the Faery Stones when I was tryin' ta open the doorway to the Fae Realm." Bridei slid in front of her man. Her thick Irish brogue belied her dark looks. She appeared more Hispanic or Italian than Irish.

"We thought ye dead," Riley said.

"So ye left her, naked in the cold instead of getting help. Cowards," Duncan spat.

"It's okay, Duncan. I'm glad. *You* found me."

God only knew what the pirates would've done to Claire if they'd taken her back to *the Fancy Seer* with them. She shuddered and moved closer to her husband.

Duncan wrapped his arm around her shoulders,

but his expression hardened as his eyes rested on the seer. "Take me ta the Faery Stones. Now."

chapter fourteen

Claire stayed close to Duncan as their party scoured the beach. All the rocks looked the same to her, but her husband seemed to know where he was going.

She couldn't even spot the ridge where Duncan, his father and Angus had first found her.

Bridei led their party, which included about three dozen of Riley's men. The seer's boyfriend walked close to her.

At every pause in their journey — and there were a frickin' lot — their heads bent together. Their low voices failed to carry their words, and *that* was super irritating.

Maybe Bridei really *couldn't* remember the location and was leading them on a wild goose-chase.

Duncan would grunt and stare with his hand on the hilt of his sword until they moved on.

He'd told Claire they were probably planning to storm the Fae palace in search of riches, and he'd said he didn't give a damn if they did. Or got themselves killed in the process.

When they'd been on the ship, Claire should've been petrified, seeing the man she'd married holding someone up against the wall by his neck — choking him, no less—but she hadn't been. Still wasn't afraid of Duncan.

He was a mix of fierce warrior and gentle husband. He'd never hurt or kill unless it was necessary. She understood that, even though it made her *feel* the difference in their times.

However, Riley O'Malley deserved everything he got.

Bridei had admitted when she'd opened the portal and accidently brought Claire back in time, she'd never actually been able to gain entrance to the Fae Realm as intended.

She didn't know if she could do it now, either.

The seer had explained they'd been blasted with some kind of magic.

Bridei and Riley had woken on the beach, without knowing how much time had passed. They'd seen Claire naked, lying with them.

They'd searched for the Stones but couldn't find them again. They couldn't remember where they were.

Duncan suspected it was some kind of Fae protection magic.

But why can't I remember lying on the beach?

Claire only remembered running.

Thinking she was dreaming, realizing she was naked, then hearing Duncan call out. Seeing the three males up on the ridge.

She trembled.

What if Bridei couldn't get the Fae Realm open?

What if she can't find the portal to my time so I can go home?

It had been an accident.

Duncan had promised to talk to the Fae princess, Alana, about opening a gate to the future, but if the seer didn't know *how* she'd done it, would Alex's wife be able to help?

Her heart started playing twenty questions, too— as if Claire needed a devil's advocate in her own head.

She ignored her internal war regarding whether or not opening the Stones to her modern time mattered.

Didn't she *want* to stay here…with Duncan?

Just when Claire had slipped from *falling* to *in love* with Duncan MacLeod was a mystery.

Maybe she'd loved him from the start.

Or maybe that was her love of romance novels talking.

It didn't matter.

Her heart skipped, then went into overdrive.

She loved this man, this giant warrior from the past—more than anything.

And you're going to walk away?

"Claire-lass, are ye hale?"

His deep voice jolted her, and she tripped over a rock.

Duncan's thick arm shot around her waist. He held her up then pulled her to his side. "Sorry I startled ye."

She smiled up at him and chided herself to calm down. The pressure on her middle wasn't helping the urge to throw up. "No problem. Thanks for keeping me from falling."

"Always, *mò gradh*. Always."

But he didn't keep me from falling for *him*.

Claire swallowed against the sudden lump in her throat.

His eyes were so warm, his expression tender. He was *her* Duncan at that moment, not the hard warrior she'd seen dealing with pirates all day.

What does he feel for me?

She wanted to stand on her tiptoes and kiss him. Wrap her arms around his neck. Be up against his muscled chest, have him hold her. Rub her back in the long soothing circles like he did every night.

God, she was going to miss that when she went home to Texas.

Claire was going to miss *him*.

Emotion crept up and threatened to envelope her. Her chest ached. Every breath was a stabbing dagger.

"Claire. What's wrong?"

"My laird!" Bridei's shout went up, preventing Claire from answering.

Thank the Lord.

Duncan released Claire as the seer hollered again.

"Jesu, woman. Ye dinnae have ta yell." Her husband frowned as they made it to Riley and Bridei.

Claire snorted. She'd never heard Duncan say *woman* instead of *lass*.

"Well, what 'tis the matter?" Irritation wrapped

his words.

"I've found the Faery Stones."

The Faery Stones weren't much to look at. They didn't look like stones at all, at least not from the current view. They were what she would call a crevice, in the fragmented cliffs that lead away from the beach and crept up into a hillside.

Claire looked around at the section of sand and rock before them, but still nothing was familiar.

Why do I still have missing memories?

"This is 'em?" Duncan breathed.

Bridei practically glowed as she nodded, her dark hair shifting around her shoulders.

Claire frowned.

Does the chick want a cookie for locating something she lied about?

Her husband moved toward the split in the cliff face. Although the entrance was cave-like, it wasn't very wide. Duncan's broad shoulders blocked the view, and he'd have to duck, possibly turn sideways to enter. "Let's hie, then," he ordered. "Claire-lass, come ta me. Take my arm."

Claire scrambled forward and obeyed without a word.

Duncan was the warrior leader again.

The group of pirates let him enter the fissure first.

She heard the shuffling of booted feet behind her, smelled the sweaty bodies of male pirates. She made a face and clung to Duncan's back, slipping her arms around his waist.

He paused, but patted her forearm and walked forward, taking her with him via much longer legs.

The cavity opened up into a cavern, once they were inside, and her tall man was able to straighten. The ceiling was low. No doubt, if he reached up, he could touch it.

Riley's men poured in too close for comfort in the space.

Claire inched closer to Duncan.

Of course, in many a book she'd read, it'd been made obvious that people bathed less in this time, but all the MacLeods she'd met didn't suffer that affliction. Duncan's clan was clean and well cared for. Even if they didn't bathe daily, like she was used to, they certainly didn't smell like these pirates.

She tried not to make a face at all the hairy beards, sweaty bandanas plastered to shaggy heads, and most definitely body odor and stained tunics.

Bridei made her way to the front of the group and pointed to five clustered stalagmites on the floor of the cave.

One was perfectly centered, and the other four encircled it. About four feet tall, they each had what looked like a crystal on top of them—more like the crystals *were* the top of the formations. They shone brightly, even though there wasn't much light inside the cavern.

Like they glowed from the *inside.*

The beauty of the Faery Stones took Claire's breath, and she nixed what she'd thought outside the entrance of this place. They were ethereal and mysterious.

Real Magic?

"Faery Stones." Bridei's tone was reverent.

Duncan's strong frame shook beside her.

Claire put her arm around his waist. In turn, her husband slipped his around her shoulders and pinned her to his side.

This is it.

She swallowed. Twice.

"Open them," Duncan ordered the seer.

"Some words a caution first, my laird."

Is she going to admit she's not sure if she can do it?

If Bridei succeeded…if she opened the portal to the Fae Realm *and* to the future, which doorway should Claire take?

Can I say goodbye before he gets his brother back?

Duncan nodded, oblivious to her internal war.

"When we cross over, the Fae will likely know we're in their realm immediately. They can sense humans from great distances." The seer's voice held the confidence of someone who knew what they were talking about, but Claire didn't like it.

No one called Bridei on her inability to open the

Stones the first time she'd tried. However, the chick was charismatic — Claire had to give her that.

Every one of the pirates — including Riley, hung on to her every word.

Her huge breasts heaving in that barely-there corset couldn't hurt, either.

Claire's stomach churned, and she clung to Duncan. Was grateful for his warmth seeping into her body through her clothing.

"My grandmother told me tales of how the Stones work, and what to expect."

"Her grandmother?" she whispered.

"Is Fae." Bridei's haughty tone held pride.

Claire wanted to roll her eyes. Not because she didn't believe the seer, but because she couldn't stand the arrogance. She'd make it her mission that little Angus didn't grow up feeling *better* because he was half Fae — especially given the way his mother's people felt about *him.*

"'Tis also likely when we arrive in the Realm a' the Fae there'll be soldiers to greet us. Guards from tha other side a' tha portal. Fae Warriors are fierce an' can fly. They have wings an' magic."

Duncan's deep voice jolted Claire, and she jumped.

He squeezed her against his side, and she took a breath.

"We will attack!" Riley's shout caused his men to rally.

They all drew swords and hollered battle cries in English and Gaelic.

Tremors raced each other down her spine.

Suddenly this feels like I'm in Braveheart…or a pirate flick.

If she went with her husband and the pirates, it wouldn't be a *staged* war for an audience seeking entertainment and a good story. Spilled blood would be *real.* People who were hurt or died wouldn't get up when the camera shut off.

No camera.

Everything was *real.*

The wilds of 1672 before her eyes.

Combat.

Danger.

Not only the lives of the stinky pirates.

Duncan's life was at risk. Hers too, if she stayed at his side, like her heart demanded.

Claire gulped.

"Open the portal," Duncan commanded.

Bridei beamed.

chapter fifteen

Wind swirled around the small cave, making Bridei's skirts shift, then plaster to her legs as it rose in strength. She had both hands on the crystal that rested on the top of the stalagmite in the middle of the five.

Duncan watched her face redden with her magical and physical efforts, but other than the wind, nothing happened. He tamped down frustration and stood as still as he could, holding on to Claire's shoulders as she squeezed his middle almost too tight.

The moving air tugged at his tunic. Fabric rustled all around him, like the sails of *the Fancy Seer* at full-speed-ahead.

Surrounding pirates were staring wide-eyed, most had mouths half-agape. If they hadn't held the seer in awe before, they would now. Not just because of her physical attributes and loose favors.

"It's not working." Riley paced, the only one not frozen. "'Twas faster last time, I remember." His thick Irish brogue made Duncan frown.

"It didn't work *right* last time," Claire said. "I was brought here."

The pirate captain ignored his wife, moving faster as he crossed the small cave.

"Riley, calm. I need ta concentrate." Bridei's voice was strained, her brow dotted with sweat, her face alight from the glowing crystals.

Her lover glared, but obeyed, crossing his arms over his chest and standing close by.

"My laird, I need your assistance," the seer called without looking away from the crystal.

"Mine?" Duncan gasped.

It was rumored he descended from a line of Fae, although how Bridei had known was a mystery. MacLeod legend claimed that an ancestor some six hundred years before had married a Fae princess—not unlike his brother.

Duncan had never believed it, although his father swore it was the truth. The man had been the laird, a grandfather many times removed.

Meeting Alana had changed things—at least it had confirmed the Fae were indeed real, but he still had doubts about the old clan story, despite his brother's wife confirming it, even telling them the princess' name—which escaped him at the moment.

If he did have Fae blood, it was minute. How could Duncan help the seer who was one-quarter Fae according to her own declaration?

Claire squeezed him, and he looked down at the woman he called wife. His heart skipped when their gazes collided.

He'd made a vow to get her home—which was what *she* wished.

It mattered not that Duncan didn't want to let her go. He'd always been a man of his word.

So, if his touch would help the seer open the gate to get his brother, as well as Claire's distant future, he'd do what he could.

Even if *goodbye* was imminent.

Her leaf-green eyes were deep pools of emotion, like before Bridei had called out on the beach.

Duncan's gut tightened.

Claire must be anxious to get home.

How was he going to let her go?

The lass had wheedled her way into his heart. When it had happened, he hadn't a clue, but he cared about her.

A voice whispered it was much more, but he refused to place a word to it. Duncan never said that word to a lass in his life—maybe not even to Janey.

Besides, Claire had married him with only the promise of protection. She'd said their marriage was temporary. He'd agreed. The means to the end of a mutual goal.

A goal that finally had come to a head.

He'd benefited from her sweet body in his bed. Duncan would have to content himself with that, because if he was honest, he'd never get over her walking away.

From him.

Because it was what she desired.

He couldn't dwell on it now.

You have a task.

He had to fight for what they both wanted.

Duncan burned to taste her lips one last time but settled for a look he hoped conveyed how he felt about her.

If everything went as planned, Bridei would open the portals at the same time.

Claire could go home; Duncan would get his brother.

"My laird." The seer's voice had an urgent edge.

He reluctantly released his wife.

The moment his hands landed next to Bridei's on the crystal, the wind inside the cavern gained more strength, reminiscent of a stormy gale on the Minch. He tightened his grip as the seer's hair flew in every direction, obscuring her face.

Bridei's fingers flew over the other crystals in a pattern. When she indicated, Duncan followed her lead, touching each crystal in the order that she had.

"It's working!"

Riley's shout made Duncan jump, but he maintained his hold on the Faery Stone in the middle, only stilling when the seer did.

Popping sounds were born, one after another, growing louder and louder.

Sweat beaded on his forehead.

Bridei's face was as red as the sash around her waist, but she too held tight to the crystal.

White light shot straight up from the magic Stone,

so bright Duncan had to crush his eyes shut. His hands burned and a blast of power smacked through his whole body.

It wasn't painful, exactly, but it made his heart beat so hard his head spun, temples throbbed. Air fled his body.

"Duncan!"

His wife's shout jolted him, but he didn't loosen his hands, even as a loud pop rang in his ears.

Duncan opened his eyes.

The whole cavern shimmered and wavered as a glowing bubble appeared before them. It hovered above the ground before floating downward, stopping a few inches in the air. At first hazy, opaque, it started to clear, like multicolored clouds retreating.

The ground cover was visible. Unnatural in color, a mixture of orange and bright blue.

"We did it!" Bridei yelled, jumping up and down. Her face was flushed pink, her chest heaving. "Ye can move, my laird. We must hurry. I've no idea how long it will remain open."

Claire's hands on him made Duncan shiver. "Are you okay?"

He nodded.

She stood tiptoed and pressed her mouth to his.

He kissed her back but didn't linger as he would've liked to.

The seer was right; time was not on their side.

"How did you…help her?"

"Long story, lass. Fer a 'nother time."

She nodded, but worried her bottom lip. "There's no gate to my time."

Duncan's heart skipped at her anxious tone. "Come wit' me. We'll get my brother and his wife. Then we'll get ye home, *mò gradh*. I made ye a promise. I intend to keep it."

"Let's go! Swords at the ready, men." Riley's order elicited hollers, then both Irish and Scottish Gaelic battle cries.

Duncan let the pirates rush through the bubble-like gateway, unable to tear his eyes away from his wife.

Claire's green eyes were wide and misty.

"Stay by my side when we go inta the Realm of the Fae. I'll protect ye, Claire-lass. Like I vowed ta get ye home, I'll keep ye safe when we're there."

"I know you will. I'll help you get your brother and the princess." Her delectable mouth was set in a hard line, but her words wobbled.

He took her mouth, couldn't help it. He needed to get that look off her face. Duncan kept the kiss short, but deep. "Thank ye, *mò gradh*." He entwined their fingers and sprinted for the portal; his wife tight to his side.

chapter sixteen

Utter chaos greeted Duncan and Claire's arrival into the Fae's world.

Her husband had been right.

They had a *welcoming* party.

The Faery Stones on this side matched their counterparts in the cave in appearance, but instead of white crystals, they glowed red, like a red-alert alarm on *Star Trek*.

Menacing.

Was that normal, or because they'd intruded?

They were out in the open, too—not hidden in a cave, or on a beach—perched on a lavish dais. As if someone cut them from the floor of whatever cave they'd grown in.

Giant, winged men swooped down; huge swords drawn. The clanging of metal on metal surrounded, burning Claire's ears, and making her shake from head to foot.

Worse than any war movie she'd ever seen.

They were like avenging angels, but their wings were fairy-like. Fragile-looking and iridescent, catching the light and shining like a prism.

However, their use of weapons was definitely

more Gabriel than Tinkerbell.

One swooped down and slashed at a pirate before retreating to the air, his long black rope-like braid swinging as he flew away.

Claire winced.

Not only were the soldiers using swords, bright flashes of what had to be magic winked in and out, thrown at the pirates.

Duncan had his huge claymore drawn, and he backed them toward the line of—pink and purple trees?

The forest was riddled with unnatural foliage. Bright colors of every hue imaginable. The grass and underbrush were blue and orange. Tree trunks were from maroon to deep red, and even one kind had blue bark and bright yellow leaves. The ground was covered with pink and purple leaves. Bright, like a box of Crayolas had vomited all over the place.

"Stay behind me, lass!"

No argument from me.

Claire gripped the back of his tunic and moved her feet when he shifted his. They probably looked like they were doing some sort of demented dance as they sought cover.

The winged creatures—men, whatever—were paying no attention to her or Duncan.

Guess I should thank the pirates for that.

They were on the ground for the most part, fighting hand-to-hand and sword-to-sword with

Riley's men, taking to the air only to dive and slash. Some of them used their long braids — they all had them — as a weapon. Others used magic, and the bright flashes made her wince and want to hide her eyes.

Claire didn't want to count the men littering the ground.

There seemed to be about a dozen defenders to start with, but more were arriving, in formation in the air, like Canadian geese headed south for the winter. However, the winged men weren't moving away from the fray, they were fighting pirates to the death.

She didn't spot Bridei or Riley, but perhaps it was like Duncan had suspected. They'd abandoned their companions in search of riches.

The Fae Warriors hollered to each other in an unfamiliar-sounding language, then attacked Riley's men as a unit, including the newest arrivals.

Claire had to look away from all the *Saving Private Ryan* style blood and guts. Her stomach was queasy. She cringed as she saw a Fae Warrior run a pirate through with a sword the same size as Duncan's.

"There's the palace!" Duncan pointed.

Her eyes followed his gesture, grateful for a distraction from the battle.

A giant castle — like three or four Dunvegans loomed on the horizon. The stones — or whatever it was made of — glistened multicolored beams of light in all directions.

Beautiful, but God, it's so far.

How were they going to find Alex?

Claire blew out a breath and blinked.

Duncan gasped.

Immediately she spotted what he had. "The castle…it's gone."

"Magic, *mò gradh*."

"Dammit, what now?" Claire tightened her grip on his tunic.

"We find my brother. It might've gone from sight, but it dinnae move. We'll find it." Duncan sounded so sure.

"Okay…what about…" She gestured to the men fighting—and dying—near the Faery Stones.

"I've no issue with these Fae killing Riley's pirates."

"Karma." Claire shivered.

"What, lass?"

"It means, they'll get what they deserve. What goes around comes around."

"I understand." Duncan flexed his fingers on the hilt of his sword. He turned to go deeper into the colored forest. "Stay tight ta me, Claire-lass. No one's attacking us yet, but I dinnae be a fan of leavin' things ta chance."

A hand covered her mouth, and someone seized her from behind.

The Faery guy wrapped his arms around her and pushed off the ground.

Claire screamed as his iridescent wings pumped. They rose higher into the air, reaching the top of the unnatural pink and purple trees.

She didn't fight him even, as her back was pinned to the hard armor formed to his chest. He might drop her.

"Be at ease. I shan't hurt you." His accent was Scottish, but it was refined, every word annunciated in a way the MacLeods' words weren't.

A roar shattered the air, reaching her ears even above the din of clashing swords and yelling men.

Duncan.

She looked down to see her husband running beneath them, his claymore held high.

He was yelling something, but she couldn't make it out.

"Put me down, bring me back!"

"I need a moment of your time, my lady. Then I promise I'll return you to your husband, Duncan MacLeod."

Claire stilled in his strong grip.

How does he know that?

"I read your mind, my lady. You are not of our time. Besides, I know Duncan MacLeod."

Read my mind?

Knows Duncan?

"Aye, it's a part of my magic. I know why you've

come."

The Fae Warrior changed direction, flying downward into the multicolored trees. Instead of pink and purple, these were bright orange, pale yellow and blue.

Still unnatural.

"I prefer the colors of this realm over the muted greens and browns of the human one," the Warrior said.

"Get out of my head," Claire snapped.

"I apologize, my lady. Fae know how to block their thoughts."

"I'm not Fae."

He touched down on a wide wooden porch.

Although, they were *in* the trees.

Claire looked around, too dumbstruck to move as the tall man—Fae—whatever, released her.

The circle-shaped door was bright green and sat as if it was carved out of a trunk so wide, she couldn't see where, or *if,* it started to round. Like a hobbit shire, but *in* the trees.

Of course, fairies live in trees.

The Fae Warrior wore a smirk on his handsome face when Claire met his gaze.

"Seriously, get out of my head."

He offered a curt nod and bowed at the waist.

She watched his iridescent wings flex with the movement. They looked so fragile, but she'd witnessed firsthand they were not.

He was tall and broad, equal to Duncan. The shiny armor on his chest and arms was dark green.

Was it metal?

How do you get green metal?

His hair was pale blond and tightly braided in a long plait that fell to his waist. It was lighter in color than her own—more white-blond or platinum. His eyes were violet. More purple than blue. He was so handsome it took her breath. So beautiful it was almost…unnatural.

"Xander."

"What?"

"My name is Xander. A member of the royal guard. Specifically, sworn to protect Princess Alana. I am her bodyguard."

Claire paused. "You guard Alana?"

Xander nodded, his long braid shifting with the movement. His chest-plate caught the sunlight, making her squint.

"Why did you snatch me?" Claire glared, even though it was crazy. He had a sword as big as Duncan's sheathed at his waist, not on his back like Duncan carried his.

Her husband had warned her of the Fae Warriors' skill, so she *should* be shaking in her borrowed deer skin boots.

"I want to help you, and I am familiar with Duncan MacLeod's temper. I needed you to listen to reason before we speak to him together, and I can reveal my plan."

"What?" she faltered, staring up into his violet eyes. They were as gorgeous as he was.

Xander held her gaze. "You're here to rescue Princess Alana."

"Not really. We're here to rescue Alex MacLeod." Claire crossed her arms over her breasts.

"Laird Alex will not leave without his wife."

"You know they're married?"

"Aye, I was witness when they wed." He nodded, and his braid jumped.

She arched an eyebrow. "And…you're okay with it?"

The Fae Warrior tilted his head to one side, studying her like Duncan did when he didn't understand her words.

Claire didn't sense that was the case with Xander. His face really was almost *too* perfect. His pale skin, flawless and beardless.

"Fae don't have hair anywhere but on top of our heads," he said, as if she'd voiced her curiosity. "Although I could grow a beard if I desired." He smirked.

She frowned. "You're doing it again."

"I'm sorry. You're not afraid of me, despite that you're not from my time, and regardless of the fact I kidnapped you."

"Glad you're fascinated." She pointed at his chest; sarcasm gone as quickly as it'd been born. "Look,

Xander. You need to take me back to my husband before he finds you and kills you."

He smirked again. "To answer your question, aye, I am *okay*, as you say, with Princess Alana being wed to Laird Alex MacLeod. She loves him, he loves her. They have a son."

"You know about Angus?" Claire flushed to her toes.

Was her nephew in danger from this…man?

"Aye, I've watched over him many times. He knows me, and we are fond of each other. The lad is not in danger, especially from me, we're kin. Cousins. His parents, however, *are* in great peril." For the first time, the Fae Warrior's voice was urgent. "You must help me convince Duncan MacLeod I can help. I have a plan."

chapter seventeen

O f all the possibilities Duncan had run through his mind before entering the Fae Realm, his wife being carried off by a Fae Warrior was not one of them. Especially since he'd not gotten much of a look at the wretch.

The winged soldier had grabbed Claire from behind and had taken to the air without pause—and a great amount of stealth.

Duncan had seen only hanging booted feet and huge wings. Hadn't even caught the color of the man's hair.

Anger and helplessness washed over him as he lost sight of them over the oddly colored treetops. His sword felt heavy in his hands.

Duncan had heard tales of Fae men coming to the human realm to rape and impregnate women. He growled, flexing his grip on the hilt of his claymore. He'd chop off the Fae bastard's bollocks and feed them to him if he touched Claire.

Is he hurting her now?

His heart took a dive for his stomach.

Nay.

Duncan ran away from Riley's men fighting the Fae Warriors at the edge of the forest.

He had to find Claire.

Save her.

Kill the winged bastard.

Then he'd find Alex.

He couldn't worry that the palace had disappeared. It was here somewhere, despite being invisible to prying human eyes. When he retrieved his wife, they'd head in that direction and get what he'd come for. Duncan would figure out how to enter when he arrived.

Maybe Riley O'Malley and Bridei had already found the palace. Damn the greedy bastard pirates who had tricked him for six months.

Let the Fae decimate them.

Duncan used his claymore to whack his way through the thick pink, purple and blue underbrush, following the direction on the ground the Fae Warrior had taken his wife in the air.

It was the best he could do.

"Duncan!"

Her shout made his heart thump, and he whirled toward a clearing to his left.

The Fae Warrior landed, flexing his wings, and released Claire from his arms.

She jogged toward Duncan, arms out as if to embrace him.

He ran forward, grabbing her wrist and whipping her behind him. Duncan brandished his claymore at the thieving Fae bastard.

Then recognition dawned.

Xander?

"Wait!" Claire tugged his arm.

The soldier dropped his stance but made no move to draw the weapon sheathed at his waist.

Duncan gave the princess' cousin an ounce of grudging respect. He could've drawn down to defend himself if Duncan had actually attacked, but he hadn't. "Xander," he said.

"Duncan MacLeod. Nice to see you again." The Warrior straightened but didn't completely relax his stance.

Smart man.

"You do know each other!" his wife exclaimed.

Duncan stilled, looking from the Fae Warrior to his wife and back.

"Xander is Princess Alana's bodyguard. He wants to help us."

"I ken who he is," he told Claire. He'd met Xander a few times, and his nephew was extremely fond of the Warrior who matched him in height and breadth, not to mention in skill.

Duncan had never seen the man's wings before, and they were astounding. They looked weak, soft as the light played off them, colors everywhere, like the surface of a pearl.

They were neither, as he'd witnessed their strength when Xander had taken Claire, not to mention the man's brethren's wings at the Faery Stones.

The Warrior's white-blond braid was long and whipped over his shoulder. He must've been a soldier for years. As Duncan understood it, the longer the braid, the more powerful and esteemed the Fae Warrior.

He'd known Xander was kin to his sister-by-marriage, but he'd never taken time to study his appearance. "Ye've the look a' her." He'd only seen his brother's wife a handful of times, but he'd recognize those eyes anywhere. Deeply hued and unusual.

"I do." The Warrior nodded. "My mother is sister to her father."

"Ye are King Fillan's nephew?" Duncan gasped.

Xander snorted and crossed his arms over his broad chest.

The Warrior wasn't going to harm them—he would've already done so—and Duncan needed to trust his wife's words. Hear what the Fae man had to say. He was from this realm, if nothing else, and knew it better than they ever could.

He forced himself to breathe deeply and sheathed his claymore on his back. Duncan wrapped his arm around Claire's shoulders and pinned her to his side.

She smiled and leaned into him.

"My mother wed down, and in secret. My father is the captain of the king's guard, hence my wings. A man of great respect in King Fillan's eyes, but not good enough for a Fae princess. My *uncle* does not acknowledge the blood we share. I am Warrior. No more."

Claire frowned. "Wow. Angus, too, because of who his father is. I don't think I like the Fae."

"Classes, my lady, a caste system. Not unlike the human world. Unfortunately, most Fae see humans even lower than our lowest caste." Xander bowed to his wife and Duncan's respect for the Fae Warrior slid up another notch.

"So not all Fae have wings?"

"Nay, my lady. There are many kinds of Fae. Our magic and appearance vary. Royals do not have wings."

"Just call me Claire."

Xander smiled.

Duncan frowned.

"What?" Claire shrugged under his arm. "Don't be a grouch. Thank the man. He's going to *help* us. Our quest just got easier."

Xander wore a smirk when Duncan met his violet eyes again but squared his shoulders. "I'll help you get them out."

"Them? I came fer my brother."

"Duncan MacLeod," Xander bowed again, but his name had been said with respect. "I've been in contact with Laird Alex MacLeod many times over the months they've been here. He will not leave the realm without my cousin. His love for her has not dimmed, and neither has hers for him."

Duncan swore.

Things were already complicated. Now they were supposed to abduct a Fae princess?

The palace was leagues from the Faery Stones and the beaches of Skye.

By God, how would they get away?

"I've an answer for you."

Surprise washed over Duncan, and he stiffened his spine.

"He can read minds," Claire said. She slid her arm around his middle and squeezed.

He frowned. "What?"

"'Tis a part of my magic." The Fae Warrior shrugged, and his iridescent wings glistened in the sunlight.

"So, how're we doin' this?" Duncan demanded, half-irritated, half-impressed by Xander.

They'd already wasted much time.

"I have a plan, Duncan MacLeod."

chapter eighteen

"Nay. Absolutely, nay. Ne'er." Duncan's tone was hard. He crossed his arms over his chest and shook his head. His dark hair shifted in the wind.

"Duncan, listen to reason. He can't get you into the palace. He can get *me* in. Even *you* agreed I could pass for Fae, if I have on a maid's robe and wear the hood."

"I dinnae plan on leavin' yer side."

Xander watched them like a tennis match, but Claire ignored him. The Fae Warrior's plan made sense.

The only way they had a chance was if Duncan went after Alex in the dungeons at the same time, she and Xander went to the tower for Alana.

They had mere minutes.

"Duncan, you have the physical size of a Fae man-at-arms, as well as no wings, like me and my brothers," the Fae Warrior said.

Her husband growled at Xander, taking a step toward him. He narrowed his eyes and leaned in, trying to intimidate the tall, fair-haired man. "My wife. My task."

Claire slipped between the two males, facing her Highlander. "Oh my God. You need to back up and take a breath. Seriously."

Duncan turned his glare to her, but after a moment, his hard expression softened. "I need ye safe, *mò gradh*."

She sighed and stood tiptoed to brush her lips to his. She settled her hands on his chest when they parted, and Duncan cupped her shoulders.

The barest touch of her mouth to his wasn't nearly enough, but it wasn't like now was the time for that.

"I need to go with Xander if we have any chance at getting them both out. Think about it. See reason. It's a double assault. A smash and grab, my sister would say. Then meet up here and get the hell to the Faery Stones. Hopefully Riley's greedy ass and his guys will keep Xander's *brothers* busy."

Duncan said nothing, but those sapphire eyes bored into her.

Claire bit back *I love you* because it was on the tip of her tongue. Her heart stuttered and she fought the urge to close her eyes.

They were in danger, right?

She should tell him, shouldn't she?

What if I lose the chance?

No.

Besides, there's always my scroll.

They'd get Alex and Alana and bring them back to their son. Safely.

"Lass," her husband whispered.

"I know, Duncan. But I have faith in you. I just met

Xander, but I have faith in him, too. We'll get what we came for and go *home*."

Duncan offered a curt nod. "I married a strong lass, *mò gradh*."

"Damn straight." Claire grinned even though he wouldn't have a clue what her phrase meant.

He flashed a smile and dipped low, kissing her hard and fast. It wasn't long or deep, but it still curled her toes.

When he released her, he put his index finger in Xander's face. "Anathin' happens ta my wife, I hunt ye down. Tear those wings off an' run ye through."

Both men ignored her immediate admonition, but a smile played at Xander's lips.

The Fae Warrior nodded curtly.

Claire groaned and threw her hands up.

Men.

At least they seemed to have a mutual respect for each other.

Xander explained the palace layout, and Claire studied the intense look on her husband's face, as he committed everything to memory.

The Fae Warrior told Duncan he would cast a spell that would disguise him and Claire as Fae. Their human blood would be rendered temporarily invisible by all Fae.

He'd take them both to castle grounds and help Duncan stun a guard so he could get a uniform.

Then her husband would go into the dungeons

and get his brother.

She shuddered but told herself not to worry. The man she loved would be fine. He *had* to be. So would Alex.

Claire and Xander would go to the kitchens, order a tray of food, and go to the tower for Alana. Getting a maid's robe wouldn't be a problem, according to the winged soldier. The stores were near the kitchens.

Her only worry was she didn't speak the language of the Fae—which was close to Gaelic as both Duncan and Xander had explained.

Xander had taught her a common gesture indicating *"I'm new here, and I'm a mute,"* in case her presence was challenged, but nerves roiled her stomach.

Her words to Duncan had been confident. *She'd* believed what she'd said. Needed to cling to the sentiment.

Fake it 'til you make it, she chanted.

Claire didn't ask what would happen if they got caught, but considering Fae commonly shunned their own people for being *different*, it couldn't be good.

Probably involved dungeons, magic, and an unpleasant death.

The king had his own daughter imprisoned.

A shiver sprinted down her spine, but she looked at her husband when he whispered the Gaelic endearment.

Duncan kissed her one last time, until her stomach

fluttered, and her legs wobbled. Like he was letting Xander know he'd claimed her, but her brain was too scrambled by desire and love, to be irritated or scold him when he let her go.

Claire *wanted* to belong to Duncan MacLeod…forever.

No, you still have to go home.

That's the plan.

As soon as Alex and Alana were safely in the Human Realm, Duncan had promised he would ask the Fae princess to open the gate to the future. Neither of them wanted to count on the pirate seer.

I'll go home.

Her heart skipped.

Wasn't *home* Dunvegan Castle?

No.

Home *is my little house. In Texas.*

"Claire, we must go." Xander's urgent voice made her jump, and she met his violet eyes. His iridescent wings flexed, and he held his arms open for her to step into his embrace.

His gaze told Claire he'd read her mind. He knew of her inner struggle, but she read no judgment there.

Heat burned her neck anyway, but she shook herself and moved into the Fae Warrior.

Duncan made a noise in his throat.

"You, too, Duncan. Flight is most efficient," Xander said.

Her husband frowned. "Nay."

Irritation crossed The Fae Warrior's handsome face. "You're not the first choice of whom I prefer to hold, either."

"Dinnae read my mind, Fae."

Claire smirked.

"Come, wrap your arms around your wife. Then I will lift you both."

Doubt crossed Duncan's expression, but he tugged Claire into his chest, and she snuggled close.

"Yes, I am strong enough to carry you both," Xander said, but it sounded like a fact, not some kind of defense or brag. "When we are airborne, I will cast an invisibility bubble, and we should be at the palace in moments."

Duncan grunted but pressed a kiss to Claire's forehead.

She smiled. "I have no issue with this plan," she whispered.

I love you still hovered on her tongue, especially since she could feel Duncan's heart beating steadily against hers.

She chided herself to concentrate on the Fae man wrapping himself around them.

Claire gasped as they started to rise into the air, squeezing her arms around her husband.

Besides Xander's chest-plate against her shoulder, she wasn't holding on to the Fae Warrior at all.

Her alarm settled as his flight smoothed out.

"There's magic around us. Making us invisible

and holding us together. We won't separate until it's time."

Xander's deep voice calmed Claire even more, and she rested her head on Duncan's chest.

"*Mò gradh,*" he whispered, but when their eyes met, her husband just smiled.

Her heart slid into overdrive. The dangers of their situation fell away. The fact they were in the air in the arms of a huge man with wings became a blip in the back of her mind.

There was only Duncan MacLeod.

The man she'd married after knowing for eight days.

The man who'd melted her heart and touched her body better than any man before him.

She loved him with her whole being.

Her *soul* belonged to a man born over three hundred years before her.

It didn't matter that there was no technology.

Not even indoor plumbing or running water.

Archaic roles for women.

Duncan was here, and it was all Claire needed.

I can't leave him.

How could she walk away?

If he didn't love her back, how could she stay?

chapter nineteen

The palace was *huge*.

As Xander flew overhead; its protection spell no longer hid it from human view.

Claire lost count of raised embattlements, turrets, and towers. The stone looked like marble, but swirled colors in the air, like a magical mist.

There were armed guards *everywhere,* with wings and without — she lost count of those, too.

They landed not far from the kitchen servants' entrance.

Claire waited — literally biting her nails — for Xander to come back and get her after the Warrior took Duncan to the dungeons.

She shoved her hand in the pocket of her trews, turning the small parchment scroll in her palm. Her other pocket contained her MP3 player.

I can't leave it here. Broken or not, it could mess something up.

Claire had written out everything that'd happened to her — how she'd got to 1672, met and married Duncan. It was *her* story as best she could tell it.

She'd signed it *I love you.*

Intended to leave it for her husband. So, Duncan

would know after she left how she felt about him, even if she couldn't stay.

Couldn't be with him permanently. Or… Would never see him again.

Before they'd left Dunvegan, Claire had dashed back into Duncan's room and grabbed it out of his desk. Impulsively buried it in her pocket. Somehow having her hand on it made her feel better — for now.

She'd give it to him when the portal to the future was open.

"It's done." The Fae Warrior strode to her, taking her upper arm in a large hand, turning her body toward the wooden double doors without another word.

"What? What's done? Is Duncan okay?"

Xander paused. "Aye. The Fae guard we attacked will wake naked, with no more than a headache. Duncan should blend in well and get his brother without difficulty. He can speak a passable Fae, if challenged. He gained keys. I managed to disable the charms and spells on the doors and locks throughout the dungeon, but it's temporary. I've told your husband to hurry. We'll meet in the forest when we've seized my cousin."

"Good."

"Until we enter the kitchens, keep your head down. You're with me, and my class is higher."

"Seriously?" Claire frowned, meeting his violet eyes.

"Aye, my lady. It is not unusual for Alana's maid

to be escorted to get her meal, but servants never speak with royal guards."

"God, I thought Duncan's world was backwards."

"It is how it is. Servant Fae don't have much magic, so they're looked down upon. The more magic a Fae possesses, the haughtier they usually are."

"That's so wrong. How can you live here?"

"If all goes well, I will not any longer."

Claire paused. "What?"

"I swore to protect the princess for life. I stay with Alana. If she wishes to live with Alex MacLeod and their son, in the Human Realm — and she does — so will I. Besides, she cannot remain here and be free."

Claire smiled. "Well, Clan MacLeod will welcome you at least, Xander. Since I've been here, they've been great."

The Fae Warrior nodded, a ghost of a smile playing at his lips, but his violet eyes were somber. "The king has given Alana little choice. She'll have to run away, and she'll need protection. Her father will not release her, even though she effectively saved his life, when she told him the Irish Prince Seamus was plotting to kill him and take his throne."

"Whoa."

"She saved his life, but King Fillan is unmoved since he found out about Alex. He decided to make his daughter a widow and imprison her for the rest of her life. Fae live long lifetimes, and I cannot abide it for her, and neither will my cousin. The king would never recognize her marriage to a human. He was angry she'd run off, married Laird Alex and gave him a *bastard*."

"What happened to the prince?" She stared, raptly caught up in Xander's tale. She swallowed.

Although Claire didn't really need him to answer. She could surmise Prince Seamus probably was no longer alive.

One look at Xander's expression confirmed it before he spoke.

"He was put to death, as were the others involved in the plot, so it is finally safe for Alana to be with Alex."

He launched into a story of how Seamus had threatened to kill all the MacLeods if Alana had run away to be with Alex—which explained why her nephew had been without his mother since he'd been born.

Claire gasped. She felt so horrible for Alex, Alana, and Angus. "Wow. Just…wow." She was glad Angus would never be acknowledged by his Fae grandfather.

"My uncle's sentiments, my lady. I do not feel the same way. I respect Laird Alex MacLeod and am fond of my young cousin, Angus. At least his mother can finally be with the man she calls husband…the man she loves. Speaking of such things, I am sorry to overstep, but considering your situation, you should tell Duncan MacLeod you love him."

Claire startled.

Relax, dummy. You knew he read your mind.

"I think I'm going to have to side with Duncan and say, get out of my head, Fae."

Xander laughed.

It was a good sound to hear, despite their situation.

"I can't tell him. I've got to get back to Texas…to the future. And besides, I have no idea how he feels about me." Her pulse thundered in her ears.

If Xander had heard Claire's feelings for Duncan, what had he heard from her man?

Would he tell her?

"Forgive me. I shouldn't have revealed what I heard. Your inability to block your thoughts doesn't give me the right to invade your mind."

So, he won't say anyway.

Claire was torn between relief and pain. "It's okay, Xander. I don't want to know. I…wouldn't want to hear it from you first. If you know what I mean."

"Aye, I do. Forgive me again, but your husband calls you '*mò gradh.*' How can you doubt what he feels for you?"

"Yeah, what does that mean, anyway?"

Xander smiled. "It means '*my love,*' Claire."

She gulped.

Duncan was calling her his love?

She fought the urge to cry, swallowing against the lump in her throat.

In a daze, Claire followed Xander into the palace and silently donned the brown maid's robe he handed her. She gladly covered her head with the oversized hood.

Her stomach roiled, but she wasn't torn up over her mission with the Fae Warrior.

As soon as they got Alana, they'd meet Duncan and Alex in the woods. They'd rush to the Faery Stones.

Claire would say goodbye to the only man she'd ever loved.

She carried a tray of food. Her arms were like rubber, and she had to order them locked into place.

Claire should be tempted by the delicious scent of whatever was in the covered bowl, but her gut and throat were tight. Her tongue was heavy, glued to the roof of her mouth.

They ascended the winding stairwell in silence, Xander's boots echoing behind her with his much heavier step.

Thank God for all that cardio she'd done weekly on the treadmill because there were about two million stairs.

The farther up they went, the more her stomach decided to chime in with nerves. Sweat trickled down between Claire's shoulder blades, and she wanted to wiggle, but made herself concentrate on each stone step.

It'd be just like me to trip and topple Xander over. We'd roll down the stairwell.

"Stay calm, and we'll be fine. When you get to the top, go to the right. There are two chambers." His voice was so low she had to strain to catch his words.

Duh, 'cause if you were Alana's maid, you'd know where she was housed.

"Who goes there?" The deep voice jolted her.

She froze on the landing.

A huge soldier strode forward, a sword as big as Claire half drawn.

"Xander. I've escorted a maid with the princess's evening meal. It's been properly screened for poison."

Poison? Wow.

Claire *really* didn't like the Fae.

She kept her head down as Xander had instructed, but she could sense the Fae guard's confusion.

"Sir Xander… A maid was already—" He got nothing further out.

Xander moved too fast to comprehend, slamming the huge man into the wall with a resounding *thud.*

Claire winced at the sickening crack, as his head bounced off the swirling marble-like stone.

The Fae Warrior held the soldier against the wall, even though he appeared to be passed out. "Go. I've canceled the magic on the locks, but they're spelled to call the royal guard if tampered with. We haven't much time."

She rushed forward and kicked the door open.

The princess shot to her feet from a giant bed. She was just as gorgeous as her cousin, if not more so. Her pale hair was free and fell to her waist in long waves. She wore a deep purple gown made of a shimmery fabric that changed colors in the light.

The Fae must like that crap — it's everywhere.
Alana wore an honest-to-God jeweled tiara.
Claire scanned the room.
No one else was inside.
Good.
The place didn't exactly look like a prison, though. The four-poster bed was fit for any queen — or princess, as it was. Dark carved wood posts that gleamed with inset jewels. A chandelier hung from the tower ceiling. It was crusted with fine gems like her crown and the bed.

The wooden armoire was just as dark and shiny.
Gilded. The *whole* room.

Even the hearth and mantel had winking specks that had to be diamonds.

Whaddaya know, Riley was right.

Claire didn't give a shit. She'd come for Alana, not baubles.

She tossed the tray of food and didn't pause as it hit the stone floor, splashing stew and mead everywhere. The small loaf of bread bounced before it bumped the hearth and stopped.

Claire rushed to her sister-in-law, shoving back the hood of the brown maid's robe.

"What—"

"I'm Claire. Let's go." She grabbed Alana's arm, ignoring the princess's wide violet eyes.

chapter twenty

►► "Wait!" Alana's shout was a regal command as Claire attempted to drag the princess across the tower room.

"We don't have time!"

"I packed a bag. Been waiting for my cousin to make his move." Like Xander, the accent was refined but definitively Scottish. Her voice was smooth. Alana tugged her arm out of Claire's grip and snapped her fingers.

Her dress *poofed* into lavender trews, a dark purple leather-looking, breast hugging bodice and white tunic beneath it. A brown satchel hung from her arm.

"Handy," Claire whispered.

Guess purple is the princess's signature color. Matches her eyes.

Alana flashed a grin. "*Now* we can go. Where's Xander?"

"Dealing with your guard." Claire thumbed toward the corridor.

"Good. Where's Alex?"

"My husband—Duncan—is getting him."

The Fae princess's violet eyes widened even more. "Husband?"

"Aye." Claire nodded as the word rolled off her tongue like she'd been using it her whole life.

Alana looked even more surprised.

"Long story. We need to go."

Xander's large form filled the chamber doorway. He gestured. "Claire, cousin. Come." His voice was more urgent with every word.

As soon as Claire and Alana rushed toward the Fae Warrior, he kicked the door open to the other room at the top of the tower.

Claire tried not to notice the Fae guard slumped against the wall.

No blood visible, but was he dead?

Xander urged them to enter in front of him. There was no one inside, but its level of grandeur mirrored the other room.

Alana snapped her fingers as soon as they were in, and Xander had shut the door.

The multicolored pane of glass in the window disappeared. No muss, no shatter, just *poofed* like the princess's gown. Sunlight flowed into the now open space.

"I gotta learn how to do that. What else can you do?" Claire stared at Alana.

"We can discuss magic later. We must go." Xander wrapped his arms around them both and lifted to the air with two great pumps of his wings.

The princess didn't get a chance to answer Claire.

"I'm going to put my arm around your waist,"

Alana said as the Fae Warrior flew straight for the window.

"Okay." Claire nodded as the other woman moved closer. A flowery scent tickled her nose. Alana smelled *good*, like a fresh rose garden.

Xander muttered some unrecognizable words and increased his speed.

Claire clutched at the princess as he abruptly changed direction.

"Worry not," Alana said in the vicinity of her ear. "He's made us invisible. He won't drop us, either."

The closeness of a stranger made her a little antsy, but it wasn't like either Fae would harm her. Besides, Alana was her sister-in-law. Claire forced herself to relax. "So, can you read minds?" She cursed her shaky voice.

"Nay, but I can speak mentally. Among other things." A smile played at the princess's lips.

"Alana has much magic," Xander murmured.

"I can *blink*, as well, although my father had the tower spelled so I could not do so to leave."

"Blink?"

"Oh, *blinking* is a form of travel, I suppose. I can think about where I'd like to be and then appear there. I can't jump between realms, but I don't have to, due to the Faery Stones. It's a rare trait, but my lad can as well."

"Angus?"

Alana's face lit up as Claire said the little boy's

name. Her violet eyes sparkled. She positively glowed.

Claire could *feel* her love for the child.

"You're not wrong about that, Claire," Xander said. "That is a part of her magic as well. My cousin has empathic magic. Sometimes she projects what she feels."

"Geesh, stay out of my head."

Alana smirked.

Xander didn't answer because he hovered over their meet-up point. He landed gently and released her and the princess.

Claire looked around, her heart pounding more with every piece of unmoving foliage her eyes rested on. Her gaze darted from colored tree to colored tree.

The two Fae stood close, also visually searching the clearing.

They waited.

Every second that ticked by made Claire's stomach jump.

Xander's mouth was set in a hard line. He drew his massive sword. The *swishing* sound it made as it cleared the scabbard shot ice down her spine.

Claire clenched her fists to her sides and chided herself to calm.

Nothing's wrong.

They'll burst through the trees any second now.

Alana paced; her beautiful face flushed. Her tiara was gone, but Claire didn't stop to wonder how and when it'd disappeared.

Her gut was tight, chest aching. She swallowed. "Where're Duncan and Alex?"

Duncan growled as the fourteenth key failed to open the cell his brother was in.

"Duncan, ye've ta hurry." Alex grabbed the crystal bars with white knuckles, but Duncan didn't let it distract him.

"Yammerin' like a lass dinnae help, brother," he grumbled.

"Aye, I missed ye, too." Alex smirked.

Duncan looked up from the rattling ring of keys, only to meet amused blue eyes that matched his own. "Ye think somethin' 'tis amusin'?" he snapped.

"Laughin' is better than despairin'."

"Just a moment ago, ye were orderin' me ta free ye."

Alex sighed. "That dinnae change. Get me outta here, will ye? They'll know somethin's wrong. Alana has been freed by her cousin—and a lass claiming ta be yer *wife*? From the *future*, my wife says?"

"Aye. My wife." Duncan grunted. "I wed, what of it? An' how do ye ken about *yer* wife?"

"What do ye mean, '*what of it?*' Ye? *Wed?*"

"Are ye hard a' hearin'? I already said *aye*. I'm goin' ta strangle ye as soon as I free ye."

Alex laughed. "I'd rather ye dinnae. I'd like ta see

my wife an' my lad again."

"I came fer ye, dinnae?"

"Alana says they're ta tha clearin'. Brother, please hurry. Tha royal guard will be alerted tha magic on tha tower locks were tampered with. We've run outta time."

Duncan rattled the keys again. "They all look tha same!" He growled. "I've lost track a' which I tried. An' how do ye know where they are?"

"Alana can speak in my mind. Limited by distance, a'course." He sounded as if he inhaled. "Duncan."

Duncan met Alex's eyes. "What?"

"'Tis magic. Ye must concentrate ta see past it. The key glows blue. Concentrate, little brother."

Duncan closed his eyes and took a breath. When he looked back down at the giant ring of keys, he stared until his temples throbbed.

Finally, as if a veil was lifted from his eyes, he could see the key with a subtle blue glow. A pale aura surrounded it.

"I have it!"

"'Tis a trick ta it. I've watched the guards. Ye must turn it ta tha right, then tha left, an' rotate it completely. If ye fail in tha' order, alarms will sound."

He followed Alex's instructions, holding the key so tightly his wrist ached. Finally, *finally*, he felt and heard the lock pop.

His brother pulled the door open, flashing a grin.

Duncan sucked in another breath and yanked his twin into an embrace.

Alex hugged him back, slapping his shoulder. "Thank ye. Captivity was tiresome."

Duncan shook his head, snorting. "Took me six months ta find ye, I'm sorry, brother."

Alex, his identical twin, had always carried the same amount of muscle on his frame that he had, but his brother's chest and shoulders were much thinner.

Duncan frowned, studying the dirty plaid and leine that was no longer white. Alex's hair was stringy, in need of a good wash, and the beard on his face thick and scraggly.

Like Duncan, his brother had always gone clean-shaven.

"Dinnae look a' me wit' pity, Duncan MacLeod. I'm as braw as ever. Let us hie to our wives." Alex patted his arm and urged him out of the dungeon in front of him.

They were almost out of the maze-like place when a shout went up from behind, the voice echoing in the cavernous dungeon.

"Halt!" The word was close enough to Scottish Gaelic to be recognizable.

Duncan unsheathed his claymore and ordered his brother behind him. The rush of feet was too close to evade. He had to take care of the problem before the guard could alert more.

When the Fae guard came into view, Alex laughed.

He was as bare as a babe. It was the guard Duncan and Xander had knocked unconscious.

The Fae didn't even have a weapon.

Duncan hollered the MacLeod battle cry and rushed the guard. His pale blue eyes went wide as he knocked him over and brought the hilt of his sword down on the man-at-arm's head.

He slumped to the stone floor, blood trickling down his forehead.

"Ye dinnae kill him." Alex had one dark eyebrow arched when they made eye contact.

"I dinnae kill an unarmed, *naked* man, even a Fae guard."

"Marriage has made ye soft."

Duncan frowned and ignored his brother's jibe. He whipped the guard's armor up and off, draping it over the unconscious Fae soldier. "Let us hie ta our wives, as ye say."

chapter twenty-one

Claire yelled when the two MacLeod men *finally* burst through the trees. She rushed to Duncan without acknowledging the man behind him, throwing herself into his arms.

His mouth took hers.

She kissed him back without thought or effort.

Her heart pounded against her ribcage, and she fought the lump climbing up her throat.

Claire didn't have much time left with her husband.

When they parted, she blinked the tears away and snuggled into his chest, hiding her face against him. Didn't want Duncan to see how much this was tearing her up.

Our time together is stolen.

If Bridei had opened both portals at the same time, Claire would've already been back in modern-day Skye.

An end to my adventure, right?

She gulped, shaking against the man she'd fallen in love with.

"Weel, weel. My little brother chose a fine wife." The voice was very similar to Duncan's, and the words were wrapped in amusement.

Claire looked at Alex MacLeod—and gasped. It wasn't his scruffy appearance, or the princess plastered to his side. He did look a bit rough for wear, but six months in a dungeon would do that. He was thinner than Duncan, but the rest was unmistakable.

He also looked *exactly* like her husband. Same height. Same long dark hair. Same blue eyes. Same face, despite the thick beard Alex wore.

"Twins?"

Alana looked amused, too.

"You never thought to mention your brother wasn't *only* your brother, but your twin? You said he was older than you."

Claire felt Duncan's arm around her shoulders move as he shrugged.

He met her eyes. "Alex *is* my older brother. We shared a womb, aye. He was born first."

She rolled her eyes, and Alana giggled.

"We must get to the Faery Stones," Xander urged. "The longer we linger here, the more chance our magic will be discovered."

"I can take one person if I *blink*," Alana said, glancing at Alex.

Duncan cupped Claire's cheeks. "Go with the princess, *mò gradh*."

Panic rose from the pit of her stomach. "No. I want to stay with you." They didn't have much time left together.

"Alex an' I will go with Xander, join ye shortly."

"*Blinking* is fast and undetectable. You'll be safe with me." Alana's voice was soft, but Claire had trouble taking reassurance from the sincere violet eyes locked with hers.

Duncan kissed her hard and fast. "I'll see ye in moments, Claire-lass."

Claire's vision blurred, but she forced a nod.

Alex tugged Alana to him and kissed her. It lingered and made Claire feel like a voyeur, but she couldn't tear her eyes away from a man who resembled Duncan so much; it was like watching her husband kiss someone else.

They stayed close, foreheads together after they parted. Alex whispered something to her, and Claire caught a word that sounded close to *gradh*.

Probably telling her he loves her.

Claire's gut clenched. Words she'd never heard from Duncan.

Should she bare her heart before she left?

It won't matter.

The scroll would have to be enough.

She ignored the smile on the Fae princess's face and her pretty pink cheeks as Alana came to her side.

"Take my hand and hold on tight," Alana instructed.

"What's going to happen?"

"You can help me by thinking about the Faery Stones. Do you remember what they look like on this side?"

"Yes."

"Good. Close your eyes and picture them. We'll be there in seconds." The princess entwined their fingers and Claire tried to convince herself *tight* didn't need to mean *death grip.* "Claire, breathe deep with me. It'll help."

She didn't have a chance to ask *help what?*

Wild bright colors flashed in her mind, like the trees in the forest were in a twirling kaleidoscope. She squinted, then smashed her eyes shut.

Then it was gone.

Claire's knees buckled and her ass hit hard ground. She could hear the clash of metal on metal.

Then men yelling.

"Claire, are you all right?" Alana's voice had an urgent edge, and she felt soft hands on her cheeks.

She pried her eyes open and met concerned violet ones. "Aye." The word came out as a croak.

"You must stand. We need to move."

Her legs wobbled when she tried to make them work, so Claire didn't push away Alana's helping hands.

Fae and the pirates were still fighting.

How much time had passed?

Dead and injured littered the ground—only pirates from what Claire could tell, but the flying Fae Warriors hovered in the air and dove after fleeing men.

"Come, lass." Alana took Claire's hand, and they sprinted to the far side of the platform the Faery Stones were perched on. "I must go and turn the red glow off. It'll cease the alarm, and no more soldiers will come. Only then can I open the gate to the Human Realm."

"Okay. Does it take long?"

"Nay, but there is no way to be invisible. The Faery Stones are warded against stealth magic."

"Great. So, they'll be able to see you," Claire said.

"Aye. I must be quick. Our men and my cousin will be here to defend me if necessary."

Our men.

She shivered and nodded. She dug her hand inside her trew's pocket and gripped the small scroll. It grounded her somehow.

Alana looked up at the dais and sucked in an audible breath. "I shall wait until they arrive."

"They said it wouldn't be long." Claire glued her boots to the ground so she wouldn't pace. She studied the soft deer hide.

A shout she didn't understand went up, and Alana's head whipped around. The princess gasped and slid to the edge of the platform, peeking around it.

"What? Do they know you're here?"

"Nay."

The shouts continued, and several of the warriors left the pirates they were subduing to join whoever was yelling.

Claire stood with Alana.

The princess was petite, so she could see over her shoulder. Bridei and Riley were running toward the

Faery Stones, both had satchels over their shoulders.

Fae men-at-arms gave chase.

"What are they yelling?"

"Thief." Alana didn't spare Claire a glance.

"Ah. Duncan suspected Bridei wasn't coming *home* to see long lost relatives."

The princess threw Claire a smirk.

A Fae Warrior swooped down, grabbed Riley, and sped into the air. The bag slipped from the pirate's grip, losing shiny objects as it plummeted to the orange and blue grass.

Claire gasped when the Fae Warrior snapped Riley O'Malley's neck.

The pirate slumped in the soldier's arms; he hadn't even had a chance to struggle. Then the flying Fae dropped Riley's body to the ground.

An anguished scream rose above the din of the fighting.

Bridei dropped her bag of stolen goods and pointed at the Fae Warrior who'd killed her lover.

Wind kicked up out of nowhere, like it had in the cavern on the beach of Skye.

The seer's skirts swirled, then her hair, until her skin began to glow, and the Fae Warrior's body started to contort in the air.

He fought back, flapping his wings and throwing a ball of blue light at Bridei, but it bounced off the golden glow around her.

"What the hell?" Claire muttered.

"Her magic. It's stronger here." Alana's voice was thick, as if what the seer was doing was hurting her. The princess's shoulders slumped. Her forehead was bathed in sweat, too.

"Hey, are you okay?" Claire had to shout. The wind was gaining tornado-like proportions.

"Aye, but you might want to hold onto something."

chapter twenty-two

"Something's wrong." Xander's voice was strained. His hands hovered over his middle, as if in pain.

Duncan exchanged a look with his brother. "What?"

"Magic. A huge surge. One of my brothers—a Fae Warrior—is being harmed."

"Alana?" Alex's tone had an edge of panic.

"Nay." The Fae Warrior's braid slipped over his shoulder when he shook his head.

"Let's hie ta the Stones," Duncan ordered. He forbade himself from worrying about his wife—his twin's wife, as well.

Claire and Alana were safe at the Faery Stones. Maybe the princess had even opened them. His brother's wife could defend them from pirates with magic, if the Fae hadn't defeated them all.

Alex was eying the Fae Warrior, whose face had gone green. "Can ye fly us, Xander?"

"Aye. Get close. We'll go."

His twin threw his arms around Duncan, and he tried not to make a face. "Ye need a bath."

"My wife dinnae seem ta mind." Alex smirked as Xander wrapped his arms and magic around them and rose into the air.

Duncan's spine tingled. He could *feel* the magic. "Aye, she must love ye more than I."

His brother chuckled, and despite the seriousness enveloping them, it was good to hear.

"Ye might be my womb-mate, but I dinnae remember ye e'er smellin' like *this*," Duncan muttered.

"Ye dinnae remember anathin' a'tall."

Their banter was discarded when Xander's face contorted with pain. His iridescent wings were pumping twice their normal rate.

Panic crossed Alex's face, and his brother gasped. "Yer goin' ta drop us?"

"My power—my magic—is being sucked away."

"Get as close as ye can ta tha ground, we'll roll." Duncan tamped down the fear churning his belly.

Xander nodded. Sweat poured from his forehead and his arms shook around them.

"Tagether?" Alex asked.

Duncan met his twin's blue eyes. "Aye. Count."

"One…two…"

Before *three* exited his mouth, Xander hovered about six feet off the ground. He released them with a groan, and Duncan lost sight of them both as he tucked and rolled into the oddly colored grass.

"Xander!" The shout was Alana's.

The Fae Warrior crumpled to the ground, unmoving. His wings were wound around his body, like a tight plaid.

They all reached the fallen Warrior at the same time.

The wind whipped around them, throwing Duncan's hair in his face and eyes, buffeting his clothes.

"I'm fine, cousin." The Fae man didn't sound so as he forced words loud enough to be heard over the rushing air.

"What's happenin'?" Duncan asked as he and Alex managed to get Xander to his feet.

"Riley was killed by a Fae Warrior," Claire said. Her warm hand landed on his forearm. "She…kinda went tornado."

Thank Jesus she's all right.

It didn't matter that Duncan hadn't exactly comprehended her statement. He grabbed her hand and kissed her knuckles, but then helped his brother support Xander.

"Open the Stones, *mò chridhe*," Alex told Alana, slipping his arm around the Fae Warrior's middle.

"I'm weak, my love." Her voice was heavy, strained, like her cousin's had been. "But I will try."

Bodies of pirates littered the area, but all the winged Fae Warriors were crumpled to the ground, their wings wrapped around their forms as they writhed in obvious agony.

The pirate seer was so radiant, Duncan couldn't look at her.

"Help her, Laird Alex. I'm fine," Xander choked out.

Duncan followed his gaze; Alana was having trouble getting up onto the platform.

His twin nodded and dashed to his wife.

Claire took Alex's place, supporting Xander with her arm around his waist. "We've gotta get outta here, Duncan. I don't want to die."

"We won't die, *mò gradh*," he grunted. Duncan wanted to touch her, kiss her, but they needed to help the Fae man who'd helped them.

Claire said nothing. However, even if his wife had intended to answer, it wouldn't have mattered.

The popping sound he'd heard in the cavern on Skye sounded in a sequence. His brother's wife must have succeeded.

"Let us hie ta tha dais," Duncan said.

Xander nodded, helping Duncan and Claire support his weight.

Wind picked up speed, pushing and pulling at their bodies as they moved closer to the Faery Stones.

The circular hazy portal was visible, but Duncan couldn't make out Skye on the other side just yet.

Alex had his wife by the hand in front of the portal, and he gestured wildly for them to pick up their speed.

Duncan couldn't see, his hair whipped into his face, and he didn't have a free hand to push it away.

Putting one boot in front of the other, he concentrated on walking forward. With every step, his legs weighed more.

The next step made no contact with the colorful

groundcover.

Pressure sucked at his limbs and plastered his clothing to his body. Duncan flailed, lost control of his feet.

Then Xander was ripped from beneath his arm.

Claire screamed.

Everything whirled in front of his eyes until his temples ached.

Then it all went black.

When Duncan came to, his wife's soft hands were cupping his face. She had tears in her eyes. "I have to go."

He sat up when Claire glanced over her shoulder.

They were on the beaches of Skye, not inside the cavern containing the Faery Stones, but the fissure-like entrance was visible behind the lass from the future who'd stolen his heart.

Duncan didn't look around though; he couldn't tear his eyes from his wife's leaf-green gaze. "*Mò gradh....*"

Claire smiled. "I know. I made a decision." Her gorgeous breasts heaved, as she sucked in an audible breath. Kissed him, but it was much too fleeting. "I'll be back, Duncan. I love you."

He scrambled to his feet, his head spinning, heart cantering.

Claire loves me.

Duncan reached for her, but his wife jogged away, a small parchment scroll in one hand, the item she called an MP3 player, in the other.

A blonde woman in odd clothing was visible through the open bubble, but wavering, as if the portal wasn't going to be open for very long.

When Claire stepped through it, and the gate disappeared with a *pop*, Duncan's knees buckled.

A roar shattered the sudden silence.

It took him a moment to process that it'd come from his mouth, because his throat burned.

Gone.

She's gone.

"Alana!"

Duncan's head swam as he heard his brother's shout. When he looked up, his sister-by-marriage was doubled over, hands buried in the sand to hold her body up.

Alex wrapped his arm around his wife's slender waist, and Duncan's gut clenched when his brother gathered the Fae princess into his chest.

Forcing himself to his feet, Duncan swallowed against the lump in his throat. He ignored the bloody bodies of the pirates that littered the beach. He couldn't remember *how* they'd come through the portal to the Human Realm.

He'd passed out.

Had they all?

Evidently, the Fae had rejected the dead that'd been littering the colorful groundcover.

No Fae Warriors were in sight, save Xander, who was sitting on the beach, head in hands. His wings were not visible.

Bridei wasn't anywhere he could spot, either.

Duncan strode to the embracing couple. "Get her back. Now."

Wide violet eyes met his gaze.

He cared not that the Fae princess was pale, nor that his brother wore a scowl the size of Scotland, no doubt because of Duncan's abrupt demand.

"Get—" His voice cracked. He had to clear his throat. "Bring my wife back ta me. Please."

Alex's expression softened.

Alana's eyes misted over, and Duncan's blood chilled when she shook her head, her platinum locks shifting about her shoulders. "I don't know if I can, Duncan."

"Brother—" His twin reached for him after he and his wife gained their feet.

Duncan shook his head, stumbling backwards. "Now. Please. I need—" A sob rose from nowhere and he grunted it away.

He would *not* cry like a lass, despite the pain lancing his heart.

"Open a door ta tha future, please, Your Highness." He didn't give two shites that he was begging his sister-by-marriage.

"Portals don't work that way, Duncan." Alana's voice was thick with regret.

"The seer did it. Twice."

"Aye, but I don't think it was intentional. I'm not sure what happened when Claire came to our time, but I think this time it was a result of the power the seer gathered in the Fae Realm. I also think it killed her in the process."

"Please." Duncan couldn't respond to her thoughts on Bridei. He collapsed to his knees before Alana, reaching for his sister-by-marriage's hand. He squeezed her slender fingers, imploring. He would crawl on his knees until the rocks bloodied them if he had to.

Begging.

He *needed* Claire.

Duncan hadn't even told his wife he loved her.

She couldn't know what '*mò gradh*' meant. Calling her *my love* and telling her how he felt were two different things.

Claire *loved* him. She'd told him.

"I need her back. I…need…" His voice broke on a sob he couldn't disguise but damn his family if they thought him weak.

Alex dragged him to his feet and embraced him.

He didn't fight his brother's hold. He clung to the man like a weeping bairn.

Tears coursed down Alana's cheeks. "Duncan, I'll try. I promise."

chapter twenty-three

▶▶ "Claire! Oh my God! Where'd you come from, and where the *hell* are your clothes?" Jules' green eyes—just like her own—widened when Claire all but fell into her sister's arms.

"I don't have much time." She stumbled, and her sister steadied her with hands to bare forearms. Claire didn't bother asking how on earth her sister could be right where she needed her to be, when she needed her.

Everything seemed to be happening for a reason, so Jules catching her as she came back to the twenty-first century had to be a part of that, too.

It was as meant to be as Claire and her husband.

The scroll she'd carefully written to explain everything to Duncan tumbled to the sand with her MP3 player. It was addressed to her husband, but Jules could read it and understand just as well.

Alana had told her whatever items were in her hands, she'd bring through time with her. The princess didn't know why it wasn't the same for clothing, especially since traveling between the Fae and Human Realms didn't leave one naked.

Panic threatened to overtake Claire when the

portal closed with a *pop*.

No. Alana will come for me. She'll figure out a way.

I will *see Duncan again.*

Claire had to. She'd promised her husband she'd be back.

Her place was at Duncan's side.

"Claire. Look at me. What's going on?" her sister demanded.

"It's unbelievable. But it's all on the scroll. I wrote everything out, Jules. Damn, writing with a quill is hard."

Jules' fair eyebrows drew tight, and she shook her. "I've been looking for you for *weeks*. You disappeared. I came all the way to Scotland."

"I knew you'd come for me, but I'm fine. I'm *good*. I'm…married."

"Married? What the hell, Claire?" Her sister reared back, making her honey-colored curls dance over her shoulders. Shock was stamped all over her pretty face, and her hold on Claire's arms tightened.

The wind kicked up. Sand blew around them, whipping their hair around. *Pops* filled the air, getting steadily louder.

The portal would be open in seconds.

Claire threw her arms around her sister. "I love you, Jules. Please know that."

"Claire, what—"

A ripping sound had their heads turning collectively.

The hazy opening hovered a foot or so off the ground and the wind burned Claire's cheeks, whistled through her ears.

Alana was a wavy figure on the other side. She was surrounded by the dimness of the cave.

Claire's heart galloped. At least she could see her sister-in-law. "I have to go, Jules. Be happy. I am. I probably won't see you again, but the scroll explains everything. Just know, I'm *happy*. Eternally." She squeezed her sister against her bare body, then planted a kiss on her cheek.

When their eyes met, Jules had tears spilling over.

"Thanks for coming for me, big sister."

"Always."

Mixed emotions threatened to bowl Claire over, and her legs wobbled. "I love you, Jules. But I love *him*, too. I need to go. I'm supposed to be with him."

"I love you, too. I don't understand..." Jules' grip on her biceps tightened.

"Read the scroll." Claire wrenched herself free of her older sister's arms and dived for the portal.

Like before, she landed on the beach, but this time at Alana and Angus' feet, not inside the cave containing the Faery Stones. Her mind wasn't hazy as when she'd woken up, running on the beach.

The last thing she remembered was her sister bending over to pick up the scroll, and Jules' covering her mouth with one hand.

Claire grabbed her stomach and sobbed.

Alana covered her shoulders with a warm MacLeod plaid and Claire pushed herself to her knees, thanking the former princess in a messy, broken whisper.

She couldn't look up until she composed herself.

"Aunt Claire!" Angus shouted. The boy squatted next to her and wrapped his small arms around her. "Uncle Duncan thought we'd never see ye again. But *Mamaidh* an' I found ye!"

Claire swallowed hard and looked up, meeting Alana's pretty violet eyes. "Thank you. For bringing me back."

The gorgeous woman smiled and nodded. "Let's get you to Dunvegan."

Xander stood on the ridge watching, dressed in dark trews and an untucked ivory tunic, no wings visible. His hand rested on the hilt of the giant sword sheathed at his waist, and the wind shifted his short pale hair.

Seeing him without his long braid and wings was jarring, but Duncan had told her Fae Warriors were renowned for their plaits. If it was cut—

Xander's presence in the Human Realm must be permanent, like he'd said.

Alana's staying to be with Alex, too.

The Warrior offered a nod and a half-smile. No doubt he'd just read her mind.

Claire didn't see anyone else on the beach. Her heart tripped. "Where's Duncan?" Her voice broke on his name.

Why wasn't he waiting for her?

"Uncle Duncan's grumpy. Roarin' an' pacin', Da says!"

"Angus." Alana's admonition made the boy's shoulders droop, but he took his mother's hand when she reached for him.

"What's wrong? What'd you mean never see me again? I promised I'd be right back."

"Aye. Days ago," Angus said.

"Days? I was on the beach in my time for less than ten minutes."

"It took us a long time to find you," Alana said. "Truth be told, if it wasn't for Angus' magic, I don't know if I could have, at all. Seems full-blooded Fae can only open the gate to the Fae's Realm. A rift through time takes human blood." She rested her hands on her son's shoulders and the little boy beamed.

Claire's blood drained to her feet. "Days?"

"Aye." Alana's voice dropped and she nodded, her pale locks shifting. "Alex finally convinced Duncan to return to the castle to bathe and eat. It's been four days, Claire."

"Oh my God. I have to get to him!"

Duncan thought I wasn't coming back.

Although he hadn't told her how he felt about her, Claire didn't regret baring her heart before she stepped through the portal to go to modern-day Skye.

She sprinted down the beach.

Away from the cave of the Faery Stones.

Away from her new family.

Claire had to get to Duncan.

She let go of the plaid because she could run faster unencumbered. Her legs burned as she scrambled up the incline of the cliff. She ignored the ache in her thighs and knees, pushing her feet harder to take her to Dunvegan.

Angus called something but she ignored her little nephew, too.

She ran as fast as she could.

Claire passed through the gates. Disregarded the MacLeod guards shouting after her. She jogged through the bailey.

Her bare feet stung as they hit actual stone flooring, but the smoother surface enabled her to move even faster than the outside terrain.

"Duncan!" Her voice echoed, bouncing around the nearly empty great hall.

He was with his father and brother, sitting at one of the long tables, his head down, long dark hair wet and curtaining his face.

"Duncan!" Claire's second shout brought his head up.

Their gazes locked.

His eyes widened.

She didn't slow her pace as he shot to his feet.

Then she was enveloped in his warmth. Plastered against his hard chest.

Her man, her Duncan, was holding her again, smelling of fresh sandalwood.

"Claire-lass." Her husband chanted her name over and over. Along with, "*Mò gradh..*"

Claire's heart took off, like her feet had, but she could feel his echoing against her naked breasts. She held on tight, her tears flowing freely, wetting his leine.

Duncan swung her around and held her even closer, as if he'd just realized she was naked.

Her stomach flipped when he stilled with her in his arms, and her gaze collided with his sapphire one. His eyes were misty. "I thought I'd lost ye, lass."

"Never," she said fiercely.

"I love ye, Claire." His mouth crashed down on hers, and she kissed her husband back with all her might.

chapter twenty-four

Duncan's weight dipped the mattress when he sat on the bed, but Claire still couldn't look at him. Her tears wouldn't quit, and she didn't want him to think she regretted her decision.

Erratic emotions aside, the last week had been heaven.

Especially after he'd finally told her he loved her.

Then said it every day she'd been back.

Claire *wanted* him. Wanted 1672 more than the world she'd grown up in.

So why the tears?

You big baby.

Her daily waterfalls and queasy stomach were going to make the coming months unbearable.

Get ahold of yourself, Claire MacLeod.

"*Mò gradh?*" Her husband's huge hand swallowed her bare shoulder. He shook gently, but she buried her face in the pillow that still carried his scent.

"I'm sorry." Claire's voice was muffled, but Duncan stilled.

"Why?"

She rolled toward him, making no effort to cover her nudity.

They'd made love twice, and he was naked, too.

Duncan's gaze darted to her breasts before he met her eyes.

Claire smirked. At least she had his attention. She shrugged. "I can't stop crying, and I don't want you to think it's you. I'm so happy to be back home. I swear. The last week with you…here at Dunvegan…it's what I always wanted."

He smiled and caressed her cheek. "What's wrong, Claire-lass?"

"Before…when I came to the beach and didn't know what was going on…it wasn't *final*. Alana says she doesn't know how the portal to my time opened. She doesn't know if she can make it happen again, even with Angus' help."

"Ah." Something flashed in his eyes and Claire's stomach fluttered.

She sat up and threw her arms around his neck.

Duncan hauled her closer, stroking her hair and back as she snuggled into him. "I was hopin' ye dinnae want ta leave me again." His whisper against her forehead was pained. His warm breath shifted her hair.

She tightened her grip on him. "I don't want to leave you. Ever."

Duncan covered her mouth with his, and desire unfurled low in her belly.

Claire kissed him back, scooting closer. However, she needed to explain before he thought the worst of her. She gently parted their mouths, her breasts rising and falling into his hard pecs as they panted against each other. "I won't see my sister ever again."

Sadness crossed her husband's expression, drawing his dark brow tight. "I ken it, Claire-lass. I'm sorry. Ye have my sister. My brother. Our sister-by-marriage. My father, an' e'en our nephew."

"I know." She sighed against his mouth. "And I love your family. I'm just a bit sad for my own. Jules…she's all the family I have…had…or whatever."

Duncan nodded and held her close, rubbing her back in long soothing circles. "I'm sorry fer yer loss, lass. But I dinnae carry any sorrow tha' ye came back ta me. Those four days. Death was seemin' like a blessing. I dinnae ken how Alex endured fer years without Alana."

Claire lifted her head and met his somber blue eyes. "I'm glad you didn't do anything stupid. Because I promised I'd come back." She poked his chest.

He batted her hand away, but a smile played at his lips. Duncan grabbed her fingers and planted a kiss on her knuckles. "When tha portal closed…'twas as if a sword lanced my heart, *mò gradh*."

"Angus said his da told him you screamed like a lassie." She tried not to smile, lest she really offend him.

"I thought I'd lost ye."

"I *told* you I'd come back." Claire huffed.

"I ken it. Howe'er, when the Fae princess says she dinnae know if she can open it back up—I panicked."

"Angus said you were grumpy."

Duncan smirked. "I'm goin' ta tan that lad's hide."

"You will not." She poked him again and he chuckled.

"Are ye tellin' yer husband what ta do?"

Claire giggled and kissed him.

He groaned into her mouth as their tongues danced.

As always, she was lost to him. She gladly let one thing lead to another.

Claire moaned as her husband kissed his way down her body.

Duncan parted her thighs and teased her with hands and fingers until she was on the brink of orgasm. He then joined their bodies, making love to her slowly, worshipping her body and whispering Gaelic endearments until they tumbled over the edge at the same time.

There was no rush, no urgency. Just pleasure mixed with so much love her heart stuttered.

He pulled her into his arms after he'd cleaned them both up and Claire's stomach fluttered.

She needed to tell him the reason for her morning dizziness and upset stomach.

Claire traced his defined abs until they jumped under her fingertips, and she brushed the dark curls that led to his sex. She couldn't get enough of his body.

Duncan grabbed her hand and covered her knuckles with kisses. "I love ye, Claire-lass."

She flashed a grin. "I love you, too, Duncan MacLeod."

Silence descended and he sighed, then he laid them back into the pillows.

The fire burned warm and welcoming, the earthy scent of peat surrounding them.

Claire closed her eyes and sucked in a breath as nerves made her stomach jump. "One thing I'll always regret about my sister…"

"What, *mò gradh?*"

"She'll never see our baby…"

"A bairn?" Duncan sat up, bringing Claire with him. Her husband's Adam's apple bobbed. He blinked.

"Aye, Duncan MacLeod, I'm carryin' yer bairn."

Shock crossed his handsome face. Then he threw his head back and laughed. "Dinnae be half bad, Claire-lass."

Claire arched an eyebrow. "I tell you I'm pregnant, and all you have to comment on is my accent?"

Duncan dipped his head down and kissed her, swallowing any further protest.

She kissed him back, like she would for the rest of her life.

Seventeenth century or not, Claire was *when* she belonged.

In the arms of a man born almost four hundred years before she was.

What she had with Duncan mattered *more* than anything she'd left in the future.

Wellllll, I'll probably always miss my MP3 player.

the end

about the author

USA Today Bestselling, award winning author of romantic suspense, epic and historical fantasy romance, C.A. loves to dabble in different genres. If it's a good story, she'll write it, no matter where it seems to fit!

She's a hopeless romantic and always will be. Risking it all for Happily Ever After is what she lives by!

C.A. is originally from Ohio, but got to Texas as soon as she could. She's happily married and has a bachelor's degree in Criminal Justice.

She's always writing, and helps small business owners by writing their websites, and she loves it!

WEBSITE: http://www.caszarek.com
EBOOK STORE:

https://www.caszarek.com/ebook-store
PAPERBACK STORE:
https://www.caszarek.com/paperback-store
FACEBOOK:
http://www.facebook.com/caszarek
INSTAGRAM:
https://www.instagram.com/caszarek/
TWITTER: https://twitter.com/caszarek
BOOKBUB:
https://www.bookbub.com/profile/c-a-szarek
GOODREADS:https://www.goodreads.com/author/show/5815085.C_A_Szarek
EMAIL: ca@caszarek.com

You can sign up for C.A.'s newsletter on her website, as well as buy all her books!